HIDDEN AGENDAS

Sandy Loyd

Hidden Agendas
Copyright © 2016 Sandy Loyd
ISBN: 978-1-941267-30-1

Published by Sandy Loyd

Edited by Pam Berehulke
Bulletproof Editing

Cover design by
Kelli Ann Morgan
Inspire Creative Services

This book is a work of fiction. The characters, events, and places portrayed in this book are products of the author's imagination and are either fictitious or are used fictitiously. Any similarity to real persons, living or dead, is purely coincidental and not intended by the author.

For more information on the author and her works, please see www.SandyLoyd.com.

This book is also available in print from some online retailers.

Dedication

This book is dedicated to my writing friend of which I have too many to list. Just know that without you all in my corner, I couldn't do this. Thanks!

CHAPTER ONE

"HEY, SIMONE, wait up."

Frowning, Simone Harris swore under her breath and counted to ten. She gave a quick glance toward the conference room where twenty company directors were sipping their morning coffee, eating Danishes, and chatting with one another. They had flown in specifically for this meeting—a meeting she was to lead in ten minutes.

If only she could have made it into the room without having to deal with Adam Smith. The blood-sucking leech fed off of others' work and tended to claim their ideas as his own more often than not.

Pasting a friendly smile on her face, Simone turned. "What's up?" If she didn't circumvent his attempts, he would undermine her authority and make her look bad. The guy was definitely nipping at her heels for her job, and his interest in feasting on her projects never seemed to wane.

"Dad wants me to attend your meeting."

"Sure," she murmured, biting back a snide retort over him calling his father-in-law "Dad." Everyone knew that the man brought Adam into the company to appease his favorite daughter.

It rankled that Simone had gotten stuck with Adam. He was a lousy assistant. Having to explain the simplest of concepts concerning his role in a project several times made her job that much more difficult, as did having to watch her back to keep the knife from going in too deep when he took credit for something she did, or blamed her for his incompetence when he messed up.

Her cell phone's buzzing vibrated through her jacket pocket. Simone shifted the marketing materials she carried from two hands to one hand, reached for the device, and noted a familiar number on the small screen.

"Hello."

"Ms. Harris?"

"Yes?"

"This is Principal Wyatt over at Holly Hills Middle School." He paused. "We need you to come and pick up your daughter, Amelia."

A trickle of guilt ran down her spine as she remembered Amelia complaining of a stomachache that morning. Simone had sensed it was more about her daughter trying to get out of going to school due to a taunt from a friend on Facebook rather than really being sick. Hence, Amelia had gone to school.

"I'll have my neighbor pick her up right away."

There was another long pause. "I'm afraid a neighbor won't do. There's been an incident involving Amelia, and she's very upset."

Simone stiffened at the rebuke in his tone. In a heartbeat, her guilt turned into concern as one thought emerged. Had her daughter done something to get even for the taunt?

"What do you mean, incident? What's happened?"

"Amelia is perfectly safe, but I'd rather not go into details over the phone."

Perfectly safe? What the hell does that mean?

Her pulse raced. Her grip on the phone tightened as she inhaled a deep, calming breath.

"Okay. I'll be there as soon as I can."

When he added his thanks, she disconnected, stuck the phone back into her pocket, and rearranged the stack of papers in her hands. Glancing at the ceiling, she sent up a silent plea that Amelia hadn't done anything stupid, like bullying a student or disrespecting a teacher.

After working her way to the head of the conference table, she leaned in to Adam, who'd situated himself on her right as if he were her go-to person, which only annoyed her on top of everything else. As much as she hated handing over the reins of the meeting, there was no other option.

"I have an emergency. Think you can handle this presentation for me?"

"Of course," Adam said, practically salivating at the chance, exactly as Simone knew he would. The man had viewed her job as a choice morsel he meant to devour from the moment her boss insisted that he join her team as an assistant.

Nepotism at its best, she thought as she explained her handouts. After all, as the CEO's son-in-law, Adam never failed to use the connection to his benefit.

Yet when it came down to a choice between her job and her daughter, Simone's daughter always won. Making it work had been the hard part, and it was something she'd gotten good at over the last twelve years as a single mom.

<><><>

THANKFULLY, TRAFFIC was light, and forty-five minutes later Simone pushed through the middle school's double doors. At the front office's glass partition, she signed in and said to the woman manning the desk on the other side, "I'm here to pick up my daughter, Amelia Harris."

"Yes, Ms. Harris. Won't you please have a seat? Mr. Wyatt will be right with you."

Too full of worry to sit, Simone paced until the door behind her buzzed and Mr. Wyatt stepped out, Amelia trailing him, her expression grim and her complexion almost white.

"What happened?" Simone asked when Amelia burst into tears and fell into her arms.

"I was just going to see the baby ducks," she said in a soft, penitent voice. "Like I do every day."

"Please, Ms. Harris, come into my office where we can speak in private." He turned to Amelia. "I need to speak with your mother alone for just a moment. Will you be okay?"

"It's okay, sweetie." Simone gave her daughter's shoulder a comforting squeeze. "I'll be right back."

3

Amelia sniffed and nodded. Then she took the chair Simone had indicated.

Mr. Wyatt opened the door he'd come through just seconds earlier and held it for her before leading Simone to another door, obviously his office. He pointed to a chair in front of his desk.

"Please, have a seat."

Once they were seated, he folded his hands. With his elbows on the desk, he let his chin rest on his intertwined fingers while his serious gaze drifted from Simone to his hands and back to her again.

"First of all, I want you to know we take every precaution to ensure the safety of our students. I don't know how else to say this without being blunt. It appears there was a kidnapping attempt on your daughter."

"What?" Shocked, Simone could only stare openmouthed, trying to process what he was saying. "Someone tried to kidnap Amelia?" She definitely hadn't expected that kind of news; the school was like a fortress. "How could this happen?"

"The proper authorities have been notified as per school policy. As I said, we are very proactive in ensuring the children's safety, but this isn't a prison and the students are free to move about on the campus between classes. The incident occurred when Amelia went outside during her lunch period, which is allowed."

Mr. Wyatt hesitated. "That's when someone tried to grab her. Thankfully, her friends started yelling and caused enough attention that a teacher noticed. That, along with Amelia's kick to the man's shin, persuaded the culprit to flee the scene. He was cautious enough to stay out of our cameras' range. The police have questioned those involved, including Amelia, but they have no suspects." He heaved a long exhale and offered her a wan smile. "I can assure you we have beefed up security."

He tapped on a brown folder on the desk, pulling her gaze. "There's no mention of Amelia's father in her records." The man swallowed hard and looked uncomfortable. "Could he have orchestrated this?"

"No." Simone shook her head. "Amelia's father is dead."

To them, anyway. There had been no contact since well before her daughter's birth—when he'd signed over his rights—but she left all that out of the conversation.

Mr. Wyatt sighed. "I had to ask since custody battles are far more common than I'd like to admit. The police even mentioned something to that effect. After all, Holly Hills has never had a kidnapping attempt before today."

"I can assure you this has nothing to do with custody."

Her tone was firm, a huge feat considering the mention of a man she hated above all others. In an attempt to shield Amelia, Simone had thought it best to hide the truth about her father being a total bastard who took advantage of naive freshmen at frat parties. To add salt to an already open wound, his family had threatened her with a lengthy, expensive lawsuit, and subsequently paid her off to have an abortion. Simone took the money, left town, and never looked back. The Moorecrofts' blood money, along with a full scholarship, helped Simone give her daughter the best life she could.

The principal leaned closer, a frown forming on his face. "Thankfully, this is the last week of school. It might be better for everyone involved if you drove your daughter to school instead of allowing her to take the bus." He cleared his throat and pushed his glasses higher on his nose, making his eyes appear owlish. "I've spoken to all the teachers, and a letter will also be going out to the parents informing them to be on the alert. We certainly don't want a repeat of the incident."

"Neither do I." Just the idea that someone had almost kidnapped her daughter set Simone's heartbeat racing. Amelia was her life.

He stood and came out from around the desk. "We shall endeavor to put this horrendous episode behind us and do our utmost to ensure it never happens again, Ms. Harris. The staff at Holly Hills will remain diligent in keeping our children safe from predators."

Simone stood and shook his offered hand. "Thanks so much for watching out after my child."

Once in the main entrance, she spotted Amelia, who jumped up from her chair and broke down in tears again.

"Oh, Mom, it was horrible. I think that man was after me. I've had this weird feeling for days now that someone's been following me."

Simone wrapped an arm around her daughter. "Why didn't you tell me, sweetie?" Why would someone target her? Without releasing her hold, she led Amelia out the door.

"Mom, I've changed my mind about staying home alone all day when school's out," Amelia said as they neared Simone's yellow Beetle parked in the first visitor slot. "I know I told you I wanted to, but now I'm too scared."

Of course she was scared. So was Simone. A kidnapping attempt was scary business. What if the guy had been successful? The idea of anything happening to Amelia was enough to turn her stomach inside out.

"We'll just have to be more aware of our surroundings." Simone flicked the button on the keyless fob. After climbing inside the car, she waited until Amelia had her seat belt in place before she said, "We'll figure something out."

She had no choice but to ensure her daughter's safety. As she backed out of the spot, her mind spun for a solution to her dilemma.

Her current babysitter, who never minded Simone's long work hours, lived two doors down and was off work in time to meet Amelia's bus. When school ended for the summer, they'd planned to try the latch-key approach after Amelia had fought tooth and nail for the freedom to remain home during the day without supervision.

Last summer, a college student stayed with Amelia. Unfortunately, the girl had gotten a full-time job and wasn't available this summer.

With all that had happened, Simone didn't want Amelia home alone either, but the timing sucked. Finding someone this close to the end of the school year would be impossible.

At two thirty, more than an hour before rush hour kicked in, there were no cars in sight when Simone turned onto the highway that led home.

When she glanced into her rearview mirror seconds later, an oversized pickup truck was bearing down on her. Fast.

When the jackass rode her bumper far too long for comfort, she tried to keep the panic out of her voice as she said, "Why won't this jerk pass?" Was he doing this on purpose?

Amelia looked over her shoulder. "He's really close."

As Simone eased off the gas, the man gunned his engine and pulled out to pass.

She exhaled the breath of air she'd been holding, then inhaled sharply when two cars appeared—one in her rearview mirror and one in front of her. The one up ahead had just turned onto the narrow two-lane highway from one of the few side streets on this route.

Cringing and sending up a quick prayer, she slowed even more and swerved to the right as far as she dared to avoid a three-car collision.

Thankfully, the pickup had increased its speed enough to pass her, then abruptly cut back into her lane. Another inch closer and he'd have clipped her bumper.

"That was too close for comfort." Simone glanced at her daughter, who'd pulled a pen and notebook out of her backpack. "We should report him. Could you see his license number?"

"I only got the first three letters."

"It's better than nothing."

Simone had to completely stop in order to calm her racing heart. Her leg shook so hard, she couldn't keep the clutch engaged. The car jerked and the engine died. Just a few feet to her right, a two-story limestone wall extended the length of a football stadium—both forward and back. No telling what would have happened if that massive truck hadn't gotten around her car when it did. She shivered and tried not to think about how close it was.

Amelia wrote the letters in her notebook and then focused in the direction the car had taken, her face white with fear. She shot Simone a worried glance. "Are you okay, Mom?"

Simone nodded. Now that her leg wasn't shaking as hard, she was able to engage the clutch and restart the car. "I'm fine. It just took me by surprise that people can be that stupid and careless," she said, not letting on what she really thought.

Why would someone try to run her off the road? Did it have something to do with the kidnapping attempt? Amelia was pale enough from all that she'd already been through. There was no sense in adding to her daughter's fears.

"Honey, there are a lot of crazies out there. Even in Norcross." Part of the reason she'd picked this part of Georgia just outside Atlanta was because it was less crowded, yet the area provided plenty of career opportunities. Apparently, being less crowded didn't mean the area was safer or less competitive as she'd assumed when she first moved here.

Jerks were after her job, her daughter had practically been abducted in broad daylight, and now this. What was the world coming to?

Pulling back into traffic, she was relieved to see a few more cars on the road. She couldn't get over the notion that the incident had been more than a random act of stupidity. Before she'd spotted either car, the guy seemed intent on hitting her.

None of it made any sense.

Or maybe it was her imagination playing tricks on her. Simone couldn't be sure, but she certainly wasn't taking any chances after the near abduction, even if there was no link to what just had happened. The only thing she could think of to keep her daughter safe would be to take action.

Her street came into view. Simone made the turn and then glanced at Amelia as an idea took hold. "How about another trip to see Grandma?"

"Sure, but I thought you were out of vacation days?"

"Yeah." Simone nodded. She'd gone in the hole on vacation days over Christmas break and hadn't caught up yet. Her stepfather had died, leaving Simone's mom a widow for the second time. They'd driven to DC for three weeks to help her mom deal with her loss. "I was thinking we could drive up this weekend and I'd drive back Sunday night. Alone. You could stay for a couple of weeks." She shrugged, but didn't add it might even be for the whole summer if she couldn't find a sitter.

"You want me to stay there by myself?" Considering Amelia's look and tone, one would think Simone was asking her to walk barefoot on hot coals.

"Yes. Work with me here. I'm trying to solve our problem. I have a job." Simone placed a hand on Amelia's knee and gave it a reassuring squeeze. "It'll be good for you to get to know your grandmother better. She's a nice lady."

Lorraine Morgan *was* a nice lady. It was a sad legacy Simone had felt compelled to stay away for so long. Her dad had died at the tail end of her junior year of high school, and her mom had remarried months after Simone left DC for her second year of college. She'd never taken the time to know her stepdad before he died, no more than Amelia knew her grandmother.

Where had the time gone? Somehow, her lofty goals of remaining close to her family had fizzled when she became a single mom. But that was about to change.

Always one to see the glass as half full, she added as she pulled into her driveway, "DC is a great place to spend a few weeks. You'll see."

Today's events had opened her eyes to a few personal issues that needed fixing in their lives. Visiting her mom seemed a perfect solution for everything, if only temporary.

Happy to have a solid plan, Simone drove into the one-car garage attached to their townhouse. After collecting the mail, she met up with Amelia as she exited the car. While the garage slowly closed, she slung an arm around her daughter and guided her inside.

"And if you really hate being at Grandma's, we'll figure something else out."

<><><>

HE PULLED into the parking lot across the street from the Harris townhouse and watched mother and daughter go into their unit. When his cell phone rang from the truck's center console, he picked it up and bit back an expletive when he saw the name on the caller ID.

"Yeah?"

"Is our project completed?"

"I'll let you know when it's *completed*," he said in a deep growl.

No one liked being micromanaged, and he was no exception. Of course, that wasn't the only reason for his testiness. A bunch of middle schoolers had bested him. Otherwise, his report would be much more positive. "It's taking more time than I had planned."

He rubbed his shin where the little bitch had kicked him. The memory didn't sit well. Clenching his jaw, he squeezed the phone, picturing in his mind what he'd do when he got his hands on the girl again.

"You promised this would be wrapped up by today," the caller said. "We had an agreement."

Still rubbing his shin, he glowered, not any happier with the delay than the person on the other end. His grip on the phone eased as he forced himself to calm down. His anger had gotten out of control for a moment. How he wished he'd been able to squish that little Beetle into the limestone like the bug it was named after.

"I fully expected it to be done long before now," his caller said in a tone filled with reproach.

"Yeah? Well, unexpected complications have set in." He paused. "Here's the deal. I'm changing our agreement. Either you pay more, or I'm walking and taking my deposit with me for my troubles."

"That's outrageous. It's extortion."

"Then report me. In the meantime, find someone else to do your dirty work."

He hung up and was just about to toss the phone into the center console when it buzzed again. Without saying hello, he said, "I take it you've accepted my new terms."

He grinned, enjoying this bit of triumph. Taking care of the kid for double would make up for today. His client had few choices and, even with doubling his price, he was considered the best in the business—thorough enough not to leave a trail. It was also why he wasn't worried about having the current contract terminated. His waiting list was extensive.

"Yes. But do it quickly or I *will* find someone else." The phone abruptly went dead.

He tossed the cell phone aside and drove off. Now that his earlier failed attempt had alerted his target, the need to figure out how to accomplish the job without any added complications was the most pressing thing on his mind.

FRIDAY MORNING, Simone saw Adam when she stepped off the elevator and shook off rainwater from her coat. Her hair, now pulled back in a ponytail, was a sodden mess. She'd have to redo her makeup, but at least she'd finally made it to her office.

"Thanks for holding down the fort."

"No problem. Everything's running smoothly."

If only she hadn't had to be out of the office so much these last few days since the incident at Amelia's school, she'd rest easier. Adam couldn't be trusted. Making sure Amelia had a ride after school took all of her organizational skills.

God only knew what went on when she couldn't be here, Simone thought, slumping into her chair. Fighting rush-hour traffic was bad enough, but this morning, a heavy downpour and a flat tire had derailed her best efforts to be early.

She opened her right side desk drawer, dropped her purse inside, and locked the drawer.

Having to wait for AAA to change a flat wasn't exactly her idea of a fun start to the day, which meant it could only get better. She would have changed the tire herself if not for the deluge. As little time as she'd spent outside in it with an umbrella, she'd still gotten soaked.

The office assistant poked her head inside the door. "Mr. J wants to see you the moment you walk in."

Simone sighed and looked at the clock on her desk. It was nine forty-five, more than two hours later than her usual seven thirty arrival. Amend that—her usual arrival before she started taking Amelia to school. She grabbed a notebook and pen and headed toward his office.

"Come in, Ms. Harris," Mr. Johnson said after she'd knocked on his office door. "Good of you to finally show up." He glanced pointedly at his watch, and the frown he offered her didn't bode well for this meeting. "Have a seat." His nod indicated the chair in front of the huge cherrywood desk.

Doing his bidding, she sat and gave him her full attention. When he remained silent for several seconds, just staring at her, Simone cleared her throat.

"You wanted to see me?" She brushed a damp strand of hair from her face and met his gaze.

He inhaled deeply. "It's time we made a change."

"A change?" She crossed her fingers as a spark of hope warmed her insides.

Please let it be the promotion I was promised a year ago. Then son-in-law Adam could fall on his face while attempting to handle her current job.

"I'll be blunt. It's obvious you've been distracted lately. Thankfully, Adam has stepped up. We're promoting him to VP of marketing, and Curtis will take over as director of marketing."

Wait a minute! She was director of marketing for New Beginnings, a home-decorating company that sold merchandise online.

Simone furrowed her brow in confusion. "I don't understand."

"Your services are no longer required. You have half an hour to pack up your desk before security escorts you to the parking lot."

"You're firing me?" She stared at him with an open mouth, fighting to understand.

"If that's how you decide to play it. Or we can just say we came to a mutual understanding." Mr. Johnson's expression was resolute.

Simone finally found her voice. "Promoting Adam doesn't make any sense. I'm the person who spent the last five years creating a viable business model, and spent many overtime hours doing it." Thanks to her, the company had gone from selling low-priced knickknacks to selling anything and everything that had to do with decorating, from the kitchen and bath, to the living room and bedroom.

"That may well be, but Adam has been picking up your slack."

"No, he hasn't. I've made sure everything was in order when I had to be out."

"You were *out* an excessive amount of time this past week."

"You would be out too if your daughter had almost been kidnapped."

His scowl didn't soften one bit.

"After this weekend, the problem will be solved," she said, fighting for her job.

"It doesn't matter. By terminating you, I've effectively solved my most pressing problem." He picked up a pen and focused on the paperwork on his desk, totally ignoring her.

Obviously, the tactic was a dismissal. There seemed no other alternative than to leave peaceably, rather than make a scene.

Simone stood, and holding her head high and her back ramrod straight, walked toward the door. Nearly out of the room, she stopped and turned around.

"I didn't realize your wife and daughter had so much sway over your company."

"Oh?" He looked up and met her gaze.

"My guess is they pressured you to promote your son-in-law."

A hint of guilty surprise flickered in his gaze.

Bull's-eye! She'd hit a nerve and uncovered the true reason for her quick dismissal.

Taking a deep breath, she said, "You're making a big mistake, and your problems are just beginning."

Her *assistant* had no clue what she did, and would fall flat on his face within six weeks. If anything, the realization gave her immense satisfaction, yet that didn't pay the bills. Still, it was something.

"But I can see you're going to have to find that out for yourself." Pivoting, she strode out of his office without looking back.

By the time Simone had packed up her belongings into the large box Security had provided and had reached her car, she was shaking.

Imagine that little twerp worming his way into her job? Slamming the box on the still-damp ground beside her car, she resisted the urge to kick her tire. It might release her anger, but it wouldn't change anything. She honest to God hadn't thought Adam Smith had the brains to set her up so easily. Apparently, he was smarter than she gave him credit for.

She pulled her cell phone out of her pocket. At least now she had the time to spend with Amelia and to act on something that had been simmering in her mind for the past few days, when it became obvious she needed a change.

"Hi, Mom. I called to let you know of my change in plans for my trip home this weekend."

"I'm flexible. I'm looking forward to your visit," Lorraine said.

"What I had in mind would be much longer than a visit." Simone sighed and pushed a lock of hair out of her eyes. "I've decided to move back to DC. Amelia and I need a place to stay for a while."

The juggling act of balancing her work and her personal life this past week had drained her. To add to her stress, every time she looked in the rearview mirror, she saw black pickup trucks. No wonder her stomach was continually tied up in knots. Whether someone was following her or not, she couldn't be sure. However, she was relieved to have a plan that would solve that problem, if it was a problem too.

"You mean my babies are coming home to stay?" The joy in her mother's voice came across loud and clear.

"Yes, Mom, we're coming home."

It felt good to say it. Maybe losing her job was fast becoming a blessing if it afforded the opportunity to return to DC, a city she loved. Funny, she'd always intended to return someday. The move would be a perfect solution to all her woes.

Besides, it was time to come to grips with her past. Simone was tired of staying away like she'd done something wrong, when in reality the opposite was true.

CHAPTER TWO

THE MAN checked his watch. Ten a.m.

A week had passed since he'd last sat outside Simone Harris's townhouse. The contract had been put on hold a few days to let things cool off before making another move. It also gave him a chance to take care of other urgent business. Right now, things were pretty quiet. There was no movement at all.

He knew all about his target's job loss after calling her place of employment when she hadn't left for work at her usual time that morning. Losing a job was one of those routine busters, so the altered schedule hadn't concerned him. He would hole up too, if he couldn't work.

In time, she'd have to start looking for another position. Then she'd create a new routine. There was no way the Harris woman could watch her back 24-7.

He would wait for his chance. When that chance came, he'd strike again, this time much faster and with more control than an angry attempt to force her off the road. Only a novice let emotions rule his actions, and he was no novice. It would be wise to remember that.

By noon, he suspected their lack of movement was more than just switching routine. It was time for quick and decisive action.

As he drove away, his mind spun for a way to achieve his objective.

He returned several hours later, fully prepared to wrap up this project in a neat package. Well, not a neat package. A bloody mess was a more apt description.

Disguised as a deliveryman, he grabbed a gift-wrapped florist box and exited his vehicle. Along with the deliveryman's uniform, he'd worn his usual wig and thick black-rimmed glasses. To any bystander, he looked the part.

He rang the bell and waited. Then he knocked.

"If you're looking for Simone Harris, she's not home."

No shit. He turned toward the voice belonging to a pretty blonde, most likely a neighbor.

Giving the woman a polite smile, he said, "If I left these flowers with you, could you make sure she gets them?"

The box contained his Uzi, one untraceable to him. Leaving it wasn't an option, but asking the question always put neighbors at ease and they'd spill way too much information in an attempt to be helpful.

"They'll probably die before Simone returns. She's out of town," the blonde said, playing right into his hands.

"That does put a crimp in things." He took a pen out of his pocket and wrote something on his clipboard. "Do you know when she'll be back, so I can reschedule the delivery?"

The lady shook her head. "No, I sure don't. She just asked me to pick up her mail. She's already been gone a while."

He offered another careless smile and gave her a quick nod, but the nonchalant attitude took all of his acting ability when his insides burned with pent-up frustration.

"Thank you, ma'am. I appreciate the information."

He made it back to his truck and threw the box in the backseat with enough force to knock the ribboned lid off. The box fell to the floor in two pieces, exposing the weapon.

The man pounded the steering wheel, sick of the delays. This job had just become personal. He was going to take care of the kid, and just for kicks, he'd make the mother watch before taking care of her too.

CHAPTER THREE

E RIC COLEMAN glanced at his cell phone, noting that only three minutes had passed since his last check. He stifled the urge to tap a beat on the table, as Patti, his date, droned on and on about her sexual prowess. She obviously thought she had a live one in him, considering that her bare foot kept touching his junk.

She was definitely his for the night if he wanted to play the game.

Any other time, he would have found the exchange entertaining. But not tonight. The realization depressed him. He picked up his bourbon, finished it off in one gulp, and looked around for the waiter.

Where was the guy?

This evening out *so* wasn't what he'd thought it would be when he'd first met Patti. She seemed nice enough. He'd even met her in a grocery store, not a bar, so he'd expected her to be different from his usual pick of women. She wasn't.

Why was he losing interest in the chase?

Maybe he was maturing, as his friends kept joking about. The whole dating game now seemed futile. What's more, the tedium of going through the motions was beginning to bore him.

Eric breathed out a sigh of relief when the waiter finally appeared to set the folder with his credit card and charge slip in front of him. After adding the tip, he signed the receipt and then pushed away from the table, trying to hold in his annoyance that Patti had ordered the most expensive item on the menu and then had only eaten half of it. The least she could have done was to ask for a doggie bag and pretend to take it home for later.

Not that he cared about the expense, but it irked him to see waste. Even now, in his early thirties, he could still remember going hungry as a kid. The fact that so many went hungry while others left prime rib on the plate shouldn't bother him, but it did.

As his date sashayed in front of him, wiggling her ass in another obvious attempt to attract him, he grimaced. Everything about Patti bothered him tonight.

The valet took the ticket he held out. "I'll be just a moment, sir."

Eric nodded.

"Did I do something wrong?"

Patti's question asked in such a forlorn tone didn't ease his irritation, but he didn't need to take his bad mood out on her.

Sighing, he shook his head. "No. You're perfectly fine. I'm the one who isn't good company."

"So, this means we're not going to hook up?"

He eyed her for a long moment before speaking. "Let me ask you something. Was that all you were interested in when you agreed to go out with me?"

She laughed. "What else would I want with eye candy like you?" Her smile still lingered as she peered at him through a half-lidded gaze in a come-hither way that he might have found enticing at one time. "You have the most gorgeous bedroom eyes. And those dimples are divine. I'm dying to taste them." She draped one hand around his neck and pulled him closer. Then she stepped into his space and locked lips with him.

The shock of her actions aroused him. Hell, he was only human. As much as his body wanted to take what she was offering, his brain knew it would be another empty encounter. He broke the connection and pulled out of her grasp.

"What's wrong with friends with benefits?" she asked in a pouty voice. Her smile was pure sin. "I can assure you, I'm real friendly."

"I don't doubt that for a moment."

Thankfully, the valet eased Eric's BMW right in front of them. Using the distraction to his benefit, he opened the passenger door for Patti, then rushed around to the driver's side, trying to think of a graceful way to end the evening.

On the drive to her apartment, the silence was deafening. "About tonight," he finally said. He touched his bottom lip, wondering if he weren't the biggest fool on the planet. His mouth still tingled, yet it wasn't enough. "I'm going to have to pass."

"You don't know what you're missing."

Her comment elicited an urge to smile, his first tonight. "I have a pretty good idea, but I was hoping we could get to know each other better beforehand."

"Are you for real?"

He glanced over at her and shrugged. "Yeah, I guess I am." An interesting revelation.

When he pulled in front of her unit and stopped the car, she jerked the door open and was outside in a fluid motion. She leaned back inside.

"Don't bother walking me to the door."

Her march toward the entrance was made with head held high and shoulders back. A queen might have a more regal bearing, but not by much. How she looked so dignified while wiggling her ass like that was beyond skillful.

As he drove away, he sighed, wishing things had turned out differently.

It was his business partner's fault. If Jeffrey Sinclair hadn't found a woman like Avery to marry, Eric would still be happily oblivious that guys like them could have thriving relationships. Even Desmond Phillips, the partner with the surly disposition, had found true love with Avery's sister.

If Des could do it, how hard could it be? After all, wasn't Eric considered the charming one in the company?

What was that saying about ignorance being bliss? In this case, being informed was pure hell. It shined a spotlight on his life's choices.

Eric didn't like the person he'd become. All he seemed to attract were the wrong kind of women—those no different from his mother. Carrie Coleman spread her legs for anyone with enough money for a hit. It never made a damn bit of difference that she had a husband and a kid at home. And his father could write a book on child abuse and bad parenting. Neither parent had wanted him. Both continually communicated the sentiment as he grew up with beatings, and ugly, hurtful words that no child should ever have to hear.

Why was he even thinking about his past? Then it hit him. Patti reminded him of his mother on some subconscious level.

Damn! What an epiphany.

He sped up, as if going faster would change the fact. But it didn't. He hadn't seen his mother since she'd skipped out on the bail Eric had posted for her when in his teens. Carrie had walked out on him, never to be seen again, also stiffing him of the money it had taken him two double shifts to earn.

Good riddance, Eric had always believed, since he'd truly been better off without his mother—except she'd left him with his father, which hadn't been any picnic either.

There was definitely a link between his past and his choices. He saw that so clearly now. Yet, why couldn't he break the habit of attracting, and being attracted to, women who weren't keepers?

Worse, he had this sinking feeling that Patti was basically exhibiting the same behavior he'd been guilty of. Far too often. For the first time in his life, he saw his actions differently.

At a red light, he grimaced and glanced at his reflection in the rearview mirror. "Not good, buddy. Not good."

Self-awareness didn't sit so well in the gut.

When Eric finally pulled into his condo complex parking lot, a bright yellow Beetle was parked in the covered spot that he spent an extra hundred dollars a month to reserve.

Damn. He'd been meaning to contact the office to complain about the ongoing occurrence for the past week.

The only spaces left at this time of night were a hike from the building's entrance. Frustrated, he drove the lot twice to eventually find a spot, then switched off the ignition, and after climbing out, slammed the car door to ease his pent-up annoyance.

Rolling his shoulders, Eric started for his apartment. Finding a car in his space only added to the nails on a chalkboard screeching inside his brain that began the moment Patti opened her door, dressed to kill in a slinky sheath that left nothing to the imagination.

Once back in the confines of his condo, he looked around at the decorated space that had set him back thousands. The traditional wood tables and earth-toned hues in the upholstery and draperies definitely didn't resemble any aspect of his childhood's bleakness, but suddenly what he saw made him feel lonely. Having nice furnishings didn't make up for what he'd lacked as a kid.

Eric threw his keys in a bowl on the antique sofa table on his way to his makeshift bar, an antique sideboard at the end of the living room. He grabbed a bottle of 1792. Knowing that he could afford the fine Kentucky bourbon usually gave him an immense sense of satisfaction. But that wasn't the case tonight. He poured himself a few ounces, feeling empty and worthless. No amount of money could change that, he realized as he headed for his bedroom, also fully decorated with expensive furniture.

An armoire that had cost more than the rest of the furniture combined held a state-of-the-art wide-screen TV. He opened the double doors and reached for the remote, kicked off his shoes and plopped onto his bed, then clicked through to watch the news he'd DVR'd earlier.

Now that he was home, he could drown out memories of a bad evening and not have to think about his failings.

He wasn't Sin or Des. While all their childhoods had been tough, his friends' pasts were like a tailgate party compared to Eric's. His had been the embodiment of a dysfunctional family.

The doorbell chimed, drawing Eric out of his depressing thoughts. He glanced at his watch. Ten forty-five seemed a little late for a social call.

Without slipping back into his shoes, he padded through the hallway. When he glanced through the peephole, he swore under his breath before he unlocked and opened the door.

"Trish, this is a surprise." Still a little stunned, Eric stared at his half sister, not bothering to hide his confusion. Had his thoughts about his dysfunctional family conjured her up? "It's been what—ten, twelve years?"

"More like thirteen. But who's counting?" Trish made eye contact. "Can I come in?"

"Sure." Eric unfolded his arms and stood aside, not realizing he'd blocked the door like a guard dog protecting his territory. Sadly, when it came to his family, he'd learned from experience it was better to be safe than sorry.

Eric waited until Trish was inside before he shut the door and led her into the living room. He picked up his empty bourbon glass and held it up.

"Would you like a drink?"

"No, thanks."

Usually, his sister never passed up free liquor. In fact, he was surprised to see her sober, considering how messed up she'd been the last time he saw her. He refrained from saying so.

"I've sworn off the booze." She made herself comfortable on his sofa and added, "And the drugs. Been clean for more than four years."

"Really?" Eric eyed her, wondering at the veracity of her statement. Most of the kids he knew in high school who got as wasted as Trish had during her late teens never got the monkey off their backs. "Congratulations."

He probably should offer her coffee, but instead continued toward his sideboard. "You don't mind if I have another one, do you?"

Trish shrugged. "Go right ahead. I've learned how to control the urge when others drink around me."

If Sin or Des were recovering alcoholics, Eric would have felt guilty for the liberal amount he poured into his glass. But then again, payback was a bitch. This was his sister who'd stolen the money he had set aside for his college fund—the same sister who'd shown up high and had made a scene, embarrassing him at his high school graduation ceremony.

Still, remembering the incident only brought back more unpleasant memories from his youth when he'd let down his guard. After all, back then he hadn't seen Trish for months. His older sister was someone he'd desperately wanted to count on. Worse, he'd idolized her.

Eric had known better than to let his parents know about his extra cash, but Trish was different. Or so he'd thought until he found his stash empty. Trish was the only person with the knowledge and opportunity to steal it. Just the idea that she'd done it had hurt him beyond anything his parents had ever done to him—mainly because he hadn't anticipated it. He hadn't heard from her since his graduation. Until tonight.

Loved ones shouldn't pull shit like that, but his family had. All the time.

As a result, trust didn't come easily to Eric. The way he saw it, everyone had hidden motivations, just as Patti had had tonight—which brought him full circle. What was his sister after?

He sat across from her and swigged a mouthful of bourbon, relishing the burning sensation that also numbed his emotions. Seeing his sister wasn't easy. As much as he didn't trust her, part of him still idolized her.

After all, it was hard to forget that during those biweekly visits she'd always made sure he had a lunch when he'd gone off to elementary school. Those other weeks he'd gone without. Although only two years older, Trish had mothered him, filling a basic need when his own mother was too wasted to give a flying fig whether he went to school hungry and dirty.

Trish had once cared, until she also followed in their father's footsteps, despite having a more nurturing mother.

"Well?" Eric set his glass down on the table next to him.

Her chin notched higher. "Well what?"

"Are you going to tell me why you're here, or are you assuming I'm a mind reader?"

"This isn't easy for me." Trish lowered her head and brushed at some invisible lint on her slacks as she inhaled a deep breath.

Eric felt a twinge of sympathy for her. Hell, she'd been just as vulnerable as him, maybe more so because she was a female and had gotten mixed up in the wrong crowd. Plus, she hadn't had Jeffrey Sinclair riding her butt like he'd had. Without some kind of mentoring, girls who came from the wrong side of the tracks usually ended up pregnant, which led to being uneducated, which led to poverty and drug addiction and so on. The cycle never ended.

"Dad's in the hospital."

"So…" He smiled. "The old man is finally getting his just rewards. Karma's a bitch."

"I guess you could say that. He's had a heart attack and is in intensive care."

Trish's brown eyes, so similar to his own with thick black lashes and accented with dark brows, pleaded with him. It was like looking at a female version of himself. They both got their looks from their father, a sad legacy from a monster. Eric was reminded of the fact every time he looked in the mirror and saw in himself the man he hated above all others.

"I was wondering if you might want to visit him. I believe it will help him get better."

Eric laughed. "Now there's a twist. The old man needs something from us. And you and I both know he never gave either of us what we needed, just beatings and hate-filled lectures." He reached for his bourbon and threw back a mouthful, blocking out ugly memories of his youth. Trish had done her best to protect him when she could, which was another reason it had been hard to believe she'd screwed him in the end. "If I gave him his due, I'd let him suffer."

"Please." Trish reached into her jacket pocket to pull out a folded envelope, and held it out.

Her expression urged him to take and open it, so he did. Inside was several hundred dollars and a promissory note for the remaining amount she'd stolen from him, plus four percent interest for twelve years.

Eyebrows raised, Eric looked at her. "What's this?"

"Restitution." A hint of red touched her cheeks as Trish met his gaze. "I was too embarrassed to do this earlier when my counselor told me it was a necessary part of my healing process."

Warmth filled him and his eyes misted. He blinked, trying not to be affected, but it was impossible. "You're too softhearted, Trish. You always have been." Forgiving her was easy, but forgiving his father enough to give the man anything other than his well-earned disdain was another matter entirely.

Eric listened patiently as Trish spent a moment updating him on Robert Coleman's condition and treatment options. She finished with, "His prognosis isn't good."

"I wish I could do something to help, but there's nothing inside me that gives a damn."

"I can't believe you're that heartless."

"Toward him, yes. I am heartless. I can't be anything else when my childhood memories won't allow forgiveness. Not for him."

"He's your father. There must be some human decency inside you that will lead you to forgive him."

"Yes, he's my father and yours, and we're his offspring." If Eric could change one thing about his life, having other parents was it. "Being a parent puts much more of the burden on him, since he was an adult whose main role was to nurture his children." Not that he was any authority on raising kids, but he'd experienced enough bad parenting to recognize it for what it was. "In thirty-one years, the man has done nothing to earn the title of father, other than offer his sperm."

"Please, Eric." Trish reached out and gripped his arm. "I've learned to forgive. It was part of the process for getting off drugs and alcohol, and staying clean."

"I'll tell you what I'll do." He ripped the note in half and placed it in her hand. "We'll call us even."

She hesitated, pressing her lips together before those pleading eyes sought his again. "He's asking to see you."

Taken aback, Eric narrowed his gaze. "Why? If he's as bad off as you say, he's in no condition to beat the hell out of me."

Not that he'd been able to do that since Eric was sixteen and returned one of his punches with a right cross. His father hadn't expected it, and for the first time in Eric's life, he saw a spark of something in his old man's eyes. Hate, admiration, or fear. It didn't matter. At that point, Eric had decided his days of being a punching bag were over. His father must have caught on to his decision because he never raised a hand to him after that.

The verbal lashings, however, didn't end until the day Eric walked out and joined the Air Force at eighteen. A week after Trish had stolen his money, along with the dream of going to college with his peers.

"He damn sure won't be able to tell me what a fine, upstanding young man I've become."

"I understand. I felt the same way until therapy." Sighing, she stood. "I had to ask in order to share what I've learned." She started for the door, then turned back around. "I hope we can now be friends." Trish opened her purse, took out a card, and handed it to him. "Don't be a stranger."

Eric walked her to the door. Awkwardly, he held his arms out. Within seconds, he was hugging her. His thoughts drifted back to when Trish was the best part of his life. He'd missed her terribly over the years. It did his heart good to know they'd formed a new connection, no matter how tenuous it was.

Once she was gone, he stared a long time at the door.

Finally, he swore under his breath and headed for bed. Trish's visit had only conjured up more feelings of inadequacy. Funny, now that he had the opportunity to do something the old man needed, Eric felt helpless, tied up with negative emotion that crippled him. His father would definitely find fault with that.

Even funnier was that a tiny part of him deep inside his gut still yearned for parental love. And the most pathetic part of all was that Robert Coleman would have a good laugh over it.

CHAPTER FOUR

SIMONE ZIPPED into an empty space in the crowded parking lot. Heaving a contented sigh, she shifted into PARK and switched off the engine.

A lot had happened in the last six weeks. She had a new job as a marketing director for a beauty-supply company, Amelia agreed to stay with her mother during the day, and Simone hadn't seen any signs of a menacing black pickup truck. Well, there were lots of black pickups in the DC area, but none paid her any attention.

"I don't need new shoes." Amelia's whine drew her out of her thoughts. "I hate shopping. Especially with my mother. Only dweebs do that."

Groaning, Simone turned to her daughter. As relieved as she was that Amelia had suffered no ill effects from that day, she still struggled with patience now and then, and had to remember she was dealing with a pre-teen.

"You need new tennis shoes for camp. No more arguments, please. We'll be quick so no one sees you." Unable to resist, she added, "Look on the bright side. No one knows you yet. So what if they think you're a dweeb?"

Amelia unbuckled her seat belt. "You're spending money foolishly," she said in a voice too grown-up for a twelve-year-old. "But I'm resigned to my fate, and it *is* your money."

"Right." Simone resisted the urge to smile as she opened her door and climbed out.

Sometimes it was difficult to believe her daughter wasn't born an adult. Even as a young child, Amelia had the uncanny ability to reason—and worry right along with her mother over the finances. Thankfully, the struggle to stay solvent had eased with Simone's new position. The condo she'd been able to sublease at a bargain in a decent school district helped. The move from Georgia had solved her problems, exactly as she'd hoped. Hopefully, her townhouse in Norcross would sell quickly.

As the two walked into Target, Simone resisted the urge to hug Amelia close and never let her go. Though almost six weeks had passed since that horrible day and they were now three states away, she'd never forget her panic over almost losing her daughter. Life was precious and should never be taken for granted.

The shoe department wasn't far from the main entrance. Amelia immediately zeroed in on a cute pair of pink tennis shoes.

"You're not seriously thinking of buying shoes in Target?"

Simone glanced toward the rack of sling backs and practically had a coronary when the owner of the male voice registered. Blaine Moorecroft, the one person on the face of the earth she never wanted to see again, stood next to another man who looked enough like him to be his brother. Two women eyeing a display of trendy shoes two aisles over appeared to be with them, but Simone couldn't see their faces.

Mortified, Simone dropped to her knees. Allowing her hair to hide her face, she pretended to be engrossed in a pair of sandals on the lowest clearance rack

Amelia bounded over. "I like them. I was thinking of getting two pair since they're on sale and I'll be playing a lot of tennis at camp." She looked at Simone, her expression asking for permission. Amelia had Simone's coloring, but that's where their similarities ended. Blaine's features were stamped her daughter's face—those same blue eyes and facial structure. Simone prayed the man in the other aisle wouldn't notice Amelia.

"Sure." Simone smiled and nodded before peeking around the aisle.

God almighty. Why had she ever thought coming home would solve all her problems? She glanced at Amelia, who was too preoccupied with trying on the second pair of sneakers to notice the concern etched into her mother's expression.

Wait a minute! Where in blazes was her backbone? Simone had done nothing wrong except trust the wrong man on the worst night of her life.

She knew exactly why she'd made the move to Silver Spring—Amelia's safety. Norcross and all that had gone on the last week they'd lived there had been pushed to the back burner of her mind.

Being in DC made Simone feel safe. Being so close to her mother made her feel safe. Being this far away from a bad memory made her feel safe. And anonymous. The two of them easily blended in with the masses in this big city of millions.

Standing as tall as her five-foot-four-inch frame would allow, and unwilling to cower like a simpering victim any longer, she looked straight at Blaine.

He happened to choose that moment to glance her way. Their gazes met and held.

Caught off guard, she blinked, unprepared for the impact of staring into eyes so like Amelia's.

One of the women, dressed in a designer outfit that probably cost more than Simone made in a month, noticed where his focus had drifted. "Do you know her?"

Blaine shook his head and turned back to the small group. "No. Come on. I just remembered Kent and I have to meet Dad."

He turned and headed toward the main aisle. The three struggled to keep up, and the one woman said something to Blaine as she walked.

Simone couldn't hear their conversation, but it didn't matter. Resisting the urge to do a fist pump, she grinned.

What were the odds of spotting him this far from his old stomping grounds? In a Target, no less? He was miles away from the ritzy DC area where he used to live. Was one of the blondes his wife? Both women looked like they fit in with his kind—cold, aloof, and pretentious. Was she a liar too? Probably.

What would Blaine think if he knew Simone hadn't had the

abortion he'd paid for?

She frowned and slanted a worried glance toward her daughter. Blaine had nothing to do with Amelia. His name wasn't on the birth certificate. As far as Simone was concerned, he'd lost any and all claim when he denied raping her. And he'd lost all legal rights to Amelia after waiving them.

The Moorecrofts had also lost any and all claim when they bought Simone off by handing her a substantial check prefaced with, "This should cover your necessary expenses, with enough left over to start a new life somewhere else." Simone had started a new life somewhere else. Now she was back.

Maybe she should have filed charges despite the threats from the dynastic family. Yet she'd had no proof, and Blaine had lots of "witnesses" ready to deny her claim.

Besides, that was then and this is now.

Time and experience had stripped away the rose-colored glasses she'd worn, which had allowed such total trust in a man who didn't deserve it.

Simone had survived his attack and the humiliation that had followed, and made something of her life. She'd be damned before allowing anything the man did nearly thirteen years ago to affect her now.

Still, Simone kept a wary eye on the couple as they exited the store.

As she stared at the glass doors, her mind spun. What if he'd been responsible for the kidnapping attempt? Or what if the person who'd followed her had acted on his behalf? Why hadn't she done some investigating as to where he lived before she decided to move here? The DC area was huge, and although her rented condo was a quick walk to the Metro and a five-minute drive from her mother's house, she could have been more thorough.

No. She shook her head, refusing to believe there was a connection. In over twelve years, there hadn't been one peep from him or from his parents.

Amelia, done trying on shoes, handed the two boxes to Simone, and they made their way together for the checkout islands.

Funny how life did a full circle and landed her right back where she'd started, but with one small exception. Simone wasn't—and never would be again—that vulnerable or naive.

DC was her home. In the short time she'd been back, she hadn't realized how much she had missed her mother all those years away. Besides, Amelia needed family and her mother needed her granddaughter.

When the salesperson finished ringing up and bagging the shoes, Simone signed the charge slip and handed the package to Amelia.

"How about checking out some cute clothes?" There were several discount stores within walking distance. In another two months, school would be starting up again.

Her daughter shrugged. "Sure."

Simone kept the pace slow as they headed toward the closest store. The entire time she walked, she prayed Blaine and the blonde had already left the area.

Though Simone had every intention of staying her course, she had no idea what would happen if the man or his wealthy family ever learned the truth about Amelia.

<><><>

ERIC'S PHONE rang and, noting Scotty's name on the caller ID, he quickly answered it. "We're still on for today, right?" He checked his watch. His tennis partner was late. As usual.

"Yeah. Traffic's a bitch. You'd think people would stay home on the weekends."

"Planning, Scotty. It all boils down to planning. Traffic's a bitch all the time in this area. You know that."

"Sorry, guy. I'll be there in ten minutes."

Eric disconnected the call and rummaged through his drawer for his tennis shorts, knowing full well that the techno geek always called with an excuse when he was ten minutes out and running late.

Once ready, he grabbed his gear and headed out to the court. Along the way, he passed the yellow Beetle still parked in his space. Stifling an urge to write a note to leave on the windshield, he continued on. *Let the office handle it.* The owner was probably some belligerent twenty-something who felt the world owed it to her to park wherever. He assumed it was a she because no guy would be caught dead riding around in such a chick car—and that included his gay friends.

Scotty was just walking up when Eric arrived at the half court with a backboard where single players could practice. The area was situated between four fenced-in courts and the parking lot. A pool and clubhouse were on the opposite side, adjacent to the courts. Residents had everything right in their backyard, which suited Eric just fine.

After the two played a vigorous match, they took a break.

Eric reached for his water. "You're getting soft. I could've beaten you that last set."

"In your dreams." Scotty grinned.

Eric wiped away moisture from his brow. It was close to ten in the morning and he was sweating like a pig, but not his friend. Of course, Scotty was a few years younger, but tennis was his passion. Meaning, he played it at least four or five times a week and could run circles around Eric without breaking a sweat.

Thumping from the backboard drew his attention. He turned and watched a girl smack the ball at the wooden wall like a pro. She couldn't have been more than twelve or thirteen.

Eric motioned with his water bottle. "She's got a mean backhand."

Scotty's focus landed where he pointed and stayed put for a full minute, as he and Eric watched the girl hit shot after shot.

"Wish I could've played like that at her age," Scotty said with a sigh. "Could've gone pro and made millions."

Eric laughed at the crack. Scotty was a brilliant whiz kid who could do amazing things with a computer. Not a full partner at SPC Electronics like Eric or Des in Sin's business, Scotty was the electronics part of the name. They all had their strengths that added to the company's success. Eric could sweet-talk any potential client into giving the company a try. Des did an awesome job of dealing with security, considering the high-tech industry was competitive . . . and dangerous at times. Sin was the glue that held them all

32

together, but without Scotty, the company wouldn't have been nearly as successful, and he was compensated accordingly.

"What? The millions you've made at SPC aren't enough?"

Scotty chuckled. "It's not the money. It's the idea of doing something guys like you can't."

About to take another mouthful, Eric squinted, eyeing him over his water bottle. "Guys like me?"

"Yeah. Tall, good-looking gods with muscular builds."

"If that's all a woman wants then she's pretty shallow, don't you think?"

"Dating me for my money is just as shallow."

"There's a solution to that." Eric bit the inside of his cheek to keep from laughing. "Don't flash it around as much."

"Believe me, if I looked like you, I wouldn't have to in order to attract the opposite sex."

"Damn, Scotty, that thinking is just as warped as mine." Eric recapped his water bottle and picked up his towel to wipe his face.

"We're quite a pair, aren't we?" Scotty grabbed his racket. "Ready for another round?"

"One more set, then I've got things to do."

Eric didn't have it in him to admit one more set was all he could muster. Scotty never let up, and Eric's competitive streak wouldn't allow him to make winning easier for his opponent.

Thankfully, they were short games. After losing the fourth, Eric practically limped to the net to shake Scotty's hand. That was when he noticed they had an observer.

With her hand over her eyes, shielding them from the sun, the girl they'd watched earlier said, "You guys are good."

Eric grunted and nodded in Scotty's direction. "He is. I'm just old."

"I'm Amelia."

"I'm Scotty, and that loser is Eric."

"How about a game?" She looked directly at Scotty.

"Sure," Scotty said at the same time Eric said, "You'll be sorry."

"No." The kid had a brilliant smile, reminding him of someone as she added, "My goal is to improve."

"Wise beyond her years." Scotty retrieved the racket he'd stashed and the two walked to their respective courts.

As Eric watched her serve and earn the first point, he tried to figure out why she looked so familiar. But he quickly forgot all about his unreliable memory when she easily beat Scotty without letting him score. Eric had never seen anyone ace his friend so many times in a row. He grinned. Imagine, this slip of a girl whipping Scotty's butt in minutes when Eric usually had to struggle for any kind of lead.

The next two games grew serious as Scotty rebounded, most likely having figured out a few of the girl's tricks. By now, he was showing her some of his own.

The score was tied when a woman strode up, drawing Eric's focus.

"Well, I'll be," he whispered under his breath. Now he knew why the girl looked so familiar.

Simone Harris—at least, that was her name in high school— slowed her steps. "Amelia," she said, halting the girl's serve. "What are you doing? You were supposed to be back twenty minutes ago. I was worried about you."

With the exuberance only a kid her age could possess, Amelia bounded over to Simone, grinning the entire time.

"Mom! This is Scotty and Eric."

Both men waved, but Eric could see *Mom* was not happy about the situation.

"We meant no harm." He made a motion with his hand to indicate Scotty. "Scotty is as near a pro as anyone I've ever played, and your daughter wanted to take him on." He smiled in an attempt to ease her concern. "Amelia's damn good."

"I know that." Tossing her blond hair over her shoulders, Simone turned her back on him and focused on her daughter. "You'd better get a move on. Your lesson starts in fifteen minutes. We barely have time to drive to the court."

Simone's tone and demeanor were cold, her blue-eyed stare icy. Not much had changed in that respect. Even after more than a decade, she was still playing hard to get. Not that Eric wanted her any longer, considering she had a daughter and was most likely a married woman now. Yet there was a time when he'd have given his right arm for her to view him as someone worthy of her notice.

Okay, she was still a golden girl, only curvier. Her fair features, refined with age, only added to her beauty, he thought, watching Simone march Amelia toward the parking lot.

A moment later he saw the yellow Beetle zip by, and lo and behold if Simone wasn't driving it with Amelia sitting in the front seat.

"Figures," he said, adding an expletive.

"What?" His swearing had drawn Scotty's attention, and he was now eyeing Eric as if he'd grown another head. "Do you know her?"

"No." Not any longer—so it wasn't an outright lie.

As Eric picked up his gear and started off toward the fence, Scotty walked right behind him.

"Yes, you do, and what's more, I'd bet a month's salary that she's someone who turned you down."

Eric clenched his teeth and struggled with the urge to take a swing at Scotty. Not because his friend was laughing at him, but because he was right. During his last year of high school, Eric had held out the hope that his father had been wrong about him being a *sorry piece of garbage*, as the old man had so graciously put it.

"I don't want to talk about it."

The first thing he planned to do was move his car into his covered spot. And rather than send a complaint to the management as he'd planned, he decided to pay Simone a friendly visit.

Just because she was rude didn't mean he had to follow suit.

AFTER A week of stalking the townhouse, the man was ready to take another chance on quizzing the neighbor again. That's when he spotted the real estate agent pounding the FOR SALE sign into the ground and realized she wasn't coming back.

Although his skill was getting rid of people, he never minded hunting them down, as long as he knew the location of their habitat. With no other alternative, he had disabled the caller ID function on his cell phone and called the real estate office who listed Simone's townhouse. He'd been lucky enough to sweet-talk a clerk in the realty office into revealing that Simone had relocated to Silver Spring, Maryland, not far from DC.

Upon hearing that news, he'd relayed it to his client and at the same time had made it clear that the project would be on hold until he got more information.

Now a month later, his cell phone rang as he was leaving his rental. He snarled when he spotted the number on the screen. Finally, the call he'd been waiting for. No one was more impatient than him to get the job done, but impatience led to mistakes. He'd already made too many mistakes.

He tapped the screen before the call was transferred to voice mail. Wouldn't do to piss off the client any more than necessary.

"Do you have an address?" he asked, his voice full of all the frustration he'd held in check until now.

"Yes. Your target is now in the DC metropolitan area."

"No kidding?" He smiled. "Got an address?"

"I'll do you one better and give you her employment information too."

His client rattled off an address and the name of a business. He committed both to memory. Written notes could become troublesome if he was ever caught.

"Thanks."

"Just hurry with the job. I'm running out of patience."

"Hell, that train's left and already returned to the station as far as I'm concerned." The woman's evasive tactic had cost him time. In his business, time was money. He clenched his fist, just itching to get his hands on the bitch to make her pay the hard way.

"You're perfectly free to hire someone else," he added, but it was a total bluff on his part. He couldn't back out. Not now. Doing so would simply add to his frustration.

"You have one week."

"I appreciate it." His smile turned into an all-out grin. It would take longer than a week just to watch her routine. Then another week to plan his latest attack, this one more successful than the last. "I'll keep you posted," he said before tapping the OFF button.

CHAPTER FIVE

ERIC SCANNED the initials and last names on the mailboxes, having no idea of Simone's married name. When he spotted *Harris*, he noted the unit number. Maybe she was divorced.

The yellow Beetle was in the lot, which meant she was probably home and now would be the perfect time for his visit. If she was S. Harris.

He grinned at the memory of seeing the car parked in Mrs. O'Leary's spot, which was right next to his. The older woman was sure to complain. She complained about everything. Eric had once parked too close to the line and had received an earful about how hard it was for her to open her car door all the way with his car butted right next to hers. Despite her car resting much closer to the line than his, Eric gladly remedied the situation. From then on, he remained cautious about making sure Mrs. O'Leary had plenty of maneuvering room.

Simone's unit was on the third floor. Without waiting for the elevator, Eric sprinted up the stairs and was outside her door seconds later.

He rapped sharply, then rang the bell.

When Simone finally opened the door after the third rap, she glared at him. "Are you crazy?"

God, she was gorgeous—even when those blue eyes shot daggers at him.

"Yeah, I must be to try and do you a favor."

"By continually ringing my bell and knocking?"

Eric shrugged. "Got your attention, didn't it? After all, that's not easy." Judging by the look on her face, she was about to shoot back a retort, but he held up a hand and stopped her with, "Look, the covered spots are reserved for paying residents."

She crossed her arms and deigned to look down her nose at him. "My lease includes a covered spot. It's in the agreement I signed." She moved to shut the door, but was hampered with his foot.

"Simone—"

"Do I know you?"

"You could say that."

When her eyebrows furrowed and her expression turned more questioning, he took pity on her. For all he knew, she probably thought he was some kind of pervert trying to worm his way into her life.

"We went to the same high school. I asked you out in our senior year, but you turned me down cold."

"I don't remember . . ." Her words trailed off and more confusion clouded her beautiful face.

"Of course you don't. I wasn't very memorable."

But he'd still been a person, one wearing his heart on his sleeve, and she'd smashed it into shards with her curt no. It had taught him a valuable lesson about his place in the world.

And in a heartbeat, Eric now understood why he always went for the bimbos. They were attainable. God, what a mental mess he'd become. Well, no more.

"Anyway, back to your car. You should check with the office. I'm sure they'll help you. Right now you're parked in Mrs. O'Leary's spot, and she's not nearly as nice as I am."

He spun around before she could spot the vulnerability in his expression, and strode away.

"Wait, I remember you now. Eric Coleman, right?"

"Well, you're too late, lady," Eric said under his breath, giving her a back-handed wave.

What were the odds of his past coming back to haunt him from two directions? First his half sister and now this!

Had to be some kind of karmic justice for some of those women he'd loved and left. To be fair, most only wanted sex, certainly nothing emotional. Even if he'd possessed the ability to give more, not one of the women he'd dated could give anything of herself in return.

Damn. Figuring out all this emotional garbage was draining. He needed a drink. The thought brought out a derisive laugh. In order not to follow in "dear old Dad's" footsteps, Eric had rules about drinking this early in the day. He simply didn't do it.

Just having the desire was enough to throw him off-balance. What really stuck in his craw was that in the last twenty-four hours, reality had hit him square in the jaw, a sucker punch of a truth he hadn't seen coming.

Eric's steps slowed as he neared his front door. Right then and there he wished for a do-over, realizing he had turned out more like his old man than he'd realized.

The thought was disturbing. Very disturbing.

<><><>

THE NEXT morning, Eric spotted Amelia sitting Indian-style on the pavement behind his BMW.

"Amelia." He nodded. "What're you doing here?"

"I still have this week before I leave for tennis camp." She stood and dusted off her shorts. "I was wondering if you could give me your friend's phone number. He promised to give me some more pointers."

His gaze narrowed suspiciously. "Does your mother know about this? What about your dad?"

She pursed her lips and stared at a point past his shoulder. Finally, she looked at the ground and shook her head. "My dad's dead. My mom's afraid I'll get kidnapped."

Shocked, he widened his eyes and frowned. "By me or Scotty?"

She shrugged. "I dunno."

"Jesus, I'm sorry about your dad." What else could he say? "It's gotta be tough to raise a kid alone. I can understand her worry." *Just not about us.*

There were a lot of sick people in the world, and Eric's mom and dad topped the list. However, as Eric had discovered once he'd gotten out in the world, most people were normal folks just trying to survive in any way they could.

Simone had always seemed rational back in high school. He should know, since he'd spent far too much time and energy trying to figure out a way to get to know her better. He wanted to ask more about Amelia's dad, but at the last minute chickened out.

"So, has somebody tried to kidnap you?"

Amelia nodded. "At my last school."

"Really." A cold chill ran up his spine as one question popped out. Why? "Then I can doubly understand your mom's paranoia." It also explained her icy demeanor toward them.

"I don't like being inside all the time," Amelia said, her forlorn expression tugging on his heartstrings.

"How about I talk to your mom and get her permission for Scotty to give you a few tennis lessons?" His offer was more for him than her. He quickly realized the favor gave him another opportunity to see the lady. As pitiful as it was, there was no denying he found the idea appealing.

"Would you?" Immediately, Amelia's smile appeared, and the brilliance of it knocked him back a bit, reminding him of Simone.

Here he thought he'd gotten over his infatuation a lifetime ago, when in reality, it just got buried behind all that other emotional stuff. At least Simone was as far from being like his mom as a dandelion was from being a flower.

Eric nodded. "As soon as I get home from work."

Amelia gave him a quick hug and ran toward the tennis court.

Grinning like an idiot, Eric watched her go. He left for the office in a much better mood than he'd been in all weekend. Didn't take a genius to understand why. Just the thought of seeing Simone again brightened his day.

Besides, he reasoned, she'd said she remembered him. *Probably as a loser*, his dark side said, snickering as it made an appearance.

Ignoring the destructive voice, he stopped outside Scotty's office and poked his head through his open door. "Amelia wants you to give her some more tennis pointers. I'm going to ask Simone for permission."

"Calling her Simone now, are we?" Scotty went back to typing something into his computer. "I was right, wasn't I?"

His smug smile gave Eric the urge to bop him on the head. "I hate it when you gloat."

Why hide the truth from him? Scotty wouldn't use the information in a negative way. He'd become a true friend, especially since he was helping Eric with his dyslexia. As far back as he could remember, reading hadn't come easily to him. Thankfully, he had a good memory and had memorized enough to get by with Cs and a few Bs in high school.

"Well?" he prodded, watching Scotty continue to tap at the keys. "Can you do it?"

"Of course I can do it. Why would you even have to ask?" In typical Scotty fashion, he didn't add more.

Grunting, Eric resisted the urge to roll his eyes. "I need some idea of when you're available. That way I'll be ready if Simone agrees."

Scotty held up a finger. "Give me a minute. I don't want to lose my train of thought."

"Sure." Holding on to his patience, Eric moved to sit in the chair in front of Scotty's desk. He owed the man a lot—mainly his ability to read better.

Eric had had no idea why his reading skills were limited until Scotty had pointed it out during their trip to Vegas to celebrate Sin and Avery's wedding. Eric had played twenty-one, following Scotty's lead. Yet when he mistook a nine for a six, an observant Scotty picked up on it. At first Eric had been too embarrassed to admit the truth, but Scotty, also being the annoying geek that he was, ignored his denials and went online for solutions.

Within hours, he'd found information that helped right away, the biggest being the amber-tinted glasses Eric now wore religiously while reading. The glasses supposedly calmed his mind so the words no longer jumped all over the page. That alone had earned Scotty the right to any and all of his little jealous barbs that came out now and then.

Besides, they weren't personal. Eric recognized another tortured soul in Scotty's attempt to build himself up in his mind with his taunts. Obviously, parents weren't the only ones who could damage a person's psyche. Bullies came in all shapes and sizes.

Scotty finally stopped typing and glanced up. "Okay. What do you need?"

Sometimes, like now, Eric's patience was stretched to the limits. "Amelia. Remember her?" He repeated what he needed and why.

"Mornings or evenings. Whatever works for her."

"What about your other games?"

"I can reschedule. Amelia is too big a challenge to pass up."

"Even though she beat you? Isn't that hard on the ego?"

"No." Scotty pushed his glasses higher on his nose, highlighting the intelligence in those huge hazel eyes, more green than blue behind the lenses. "Logic never affects my ego."

"Really?" That was news to him. Eric shrugged. But what did he really know about his friend and coworker, other than what Scotty chose to divulge. Which wasn't much.

"She has skill and a gift. Logically, I'd be an idiot to let it bother me."

"I see." Eric shook his head in an effort to wrap his brain around the concept. "Just so we're on the same page, you're free mornings from seven to—" Eric glanced at him with the question in his eyes.

"Nine in the mornings and seven to ten at night."

"What about this weekend?"

"Anytime's fine."

Eric's eyebrows remained raised.

Scotty grinned. "It's only one week, right?" When Eric nodded, he added, "You and I can work around Amelia. Right?"

"No problem. I'll keep you in the loop." With that, Eric rose and strode out the door, eager to get on with his day. It couldn't pass quickly enough for him.

CHAPTER SIX

A KNOCK on Blaine Moorecroft's office door interrupted his thoughts. He opened his top drawer and stuck the report he'd been reading from his private investigator inside. As he closed the drawer and glanced up, his brother stepped into the office, strode purposefully toward the desk, and plopped into the chair in front of it like he didn't have a care in the world.

Of course Kent acted that way. He was the younger son. Their father had always insisted that Blaine, the older son, would one day run for president and fulfill the old man's lifelong dream. And so far, his plans were right on track.

Kent leaned back and propped his right ankle on his left knee.

Like Blaine, Kent had inherited his dark hair and blue eyes from their father. Both were six feet tall and had muscular builds. Blaine still kept in shape with daily workouts, but Kent complained it took too long. As a result, Kent had a slight paunch that was easily hidden in the thousand-dollar suits he wore.

"Something bothering you, bro?" Kent asked.

The careless smirk crossing his face gave Blaine the impression his brother knew Blaine's deepest secret. Yet, Kent couldn't know about Simone because their father had worked hard to keep everything about that situation contained.

And I sure as hell wouldn't tell anyone.

Forcing a nonchalance he didn't feel, Blaine gave his brother a smile. "Not a thing," he said, lying through his teeth.

"I take it you're ready for our fund-raiser tonight?"

"Yeah, all set." Blaine locked the drawer and stuck the key in his pocket.

"Good." Kent's grin widened. "All you have to do is use those Moorecroft good looks while you lay on the charm, don't screw up your speech, and let me work the crowd. I know exactly what pieces to move where on the game board."

Since Kent had already been elected to Congress, he'd taken it upon himself to act as Blaine's behind-the-scenes political adviser. Kent understood politics better, meaning he knew all the tricks for annihilating the opponent. So far, he'd done an outstanding job.

With the election only four months away, Blaine was ahead in the polls. Given the opportunity, he might have handled things differently, but it only seemed fitting that he follow his brother's advice. After all, Kent, a born politician, had always made it known he'd relish a chance at the top position in the country.

Yet when the brothers were just teens, their father had stomped on Kent's ambition. The news had crushed Kent, and from then on he'd always been a little envious of Blaine's destiny. Hell, Blaine had tried to make his father see reason. Just because Blaine was the oldest didn't mean he was the best candidate. But his pleas and arguments had fallen on deaf ears.

Moorecroft's goal was to use his sons to the fullest advantage in order to build a political dynasty to rival that of the Kennedys. According to the old man, Kent didn't have the balls to go the distance. Blaine had already proven he could, meaning he'd kept his mouth shut and done what needed to be done when a foolish mistake in college had nearly ruined his life. It hadn't hurt that he'd been president of his fraternity and had graduated summa cum laude from Georgetown.

Christ, he wanted a drink. Politics was a dirty business. The best way to numb his dark soul was a bottle of Absolut. But getting wasted would have to wait until he'd performed his duties.

Tamping down his misery, Blaine stood and straightened his tie. "I'm just glad you've got my back."

Kent jumped to his feet with the enthusiasm of a boxer ready to go a few rounds. "It's something I'm good at."

"Yeah, I know," Blaine murmured, following his brother out of the room.

Too bad their dad had earmarked the wrong son for president. Kent would have been good at that too. Much better than him.

After all, Kent didn't have an albatross named Simone Harris hanging around his neck.

Blaine smiled, wondering how Kent would handle that dirty little secret.

CHAPTER SEVEN

S IMONE KNOCKED, then using her key to open the door to her mom's house, let herself in. "Hello, where is everybody?"

"We're out on the deck."

That made sense. It was a gorgeous day. Not too hot as it usually was in late June. Depending on the weather patterns, the DC area could be like today, or hotter than Hades.

Simone wound her way through the family room toward the kitchen, following her mother's voice and the sweet sound of Amelia's laughter.

"What's going on?" She stopped at the screen door.

Her daughter, sitting cross-legged on the deck, looked up. "Hi, Mom." Something wriggled in her lap.

Lorraine chuckled. "Amelia has a new friend."

"It's a kitten, Mom." There was excitement in Amelia's voice. "Isn't she adorable?"

After sending her mother a *what the heck* look, Simone stepped outside and turned to smile at Amelia. "It sure is," she said, then cleared her throat. "Unfortunately—"

"Don't worry, honey," her mother interjected. "Buttons is mine. I get lonely during the day, and having a cat around will keep me company when Dean is on the road."

"Plus," Amelia added, "I get to visit her and pretend she's mine when I'm here during the day."

Simone knelt beside Amelia and pushed stray hairs out of her daughter's eyes, relishing in the touch of her baby-soft skin. The kitten bounded over and started tugging on the hemmed tip of Simone's blouse before going for the bottom button.

Amelia laughed. "That's why we named her Buttons. They're her favorite snack."

"She is kind of cute." Simone picked her up and studied her. "Really no more than a ball of gray-striped fur."

"How was your first day of work?"

"Awesome. I couldn't ask for a better boss." As director of marketing for the beauty-supply company, her job description was similar to her previous one, but the company was nothing like her old one. "My coworkers are great. I've met a lot of nice people. In fact, I had lunch with a nice man who was eating alone. Today was his first day at his job too, and we started chatting. I'm meeting him for lunch tomorrow."

"You actually have a boyfriend, Mom?"

The incredulous quality to the question didn't slip Simone's notice.

"Maybe."

A giggle rose up and warmth hit her cheeks. Goodness, she rather did feel like a teenager with her first crush. Dating hadn't been her thing since . . . well . . . since she got pregnant. Simone had this uncanny suspicion that being back home, within five minutes from her mother's house, gave her a sense of security she'd lacked in Georgia. In a heartbeat, she understood the full consequences of the rape. She'd no longer trusted her judgment with men. It was time to quit letting that incident define her life.

Lorraine rose and started for the house. "I'm relieved to hear such good news. Why don't you have a seat? I'll get us some snacks and lemonade, then you can tell me all about it before you head home."

"I'll help." Simone followed her mother. Inside, she moved to the cupboard and retrieved three glasses. Amelia's coos and giggles drifted in through the screen door as Lorraine opened the fridge.

"What's this guy's name? And what's he like?" Her mother flashed her a sheepish grin. "That is, if you don't mind sharing."

Simone heaved a relieved sigh. It was wonderful to be here in her mom's kitchen chatting about her day. "Michael Belk. He's nice enough."

Only now she didn't want to talk about the man she'd eaten lunch with. After chatting with him while waiting to order, she'd agreed to join him when he asked. He was in his mid-thirties, not quite six feet tall but stocky and seemed athletic, and was attractive with dark blond hair and trendy hipster glasses that framed his blue eyes. Despite his hawkish gaze that had been unnerving at first, he'd smiled a lot and seemed friendly enough, and having remembered Eric's comment during his visit last night, she'd decided it was time to be a little nicer to men she met.

Giving her mom a considering glance, Simone worried her bottom lip with her teeth. "Mom, was I a bitch in high school?"

The comment got Lorraine's attention and she turned, a totally stunned expression taking over her features. "What?" Then her gaze narrowed. "Why would you ask that?"

"I just remember being very picky about the guys I dated back then." A mistake she was trying to rectify, hence the lunch date. Ordinarily, she'd have made up an excuse.

"Yes, I recall you mentioning something about that when I'd ask about the boys who called you. Right after your father died." A sad frown appeared. "To be honest, I wasn't much of a mother that year, and didn't notice much."

"We were grieving," Simone said softly.

Hugging herself, she thought back to high school and those painful months after her dad died. She'd been Joshua Harris's darling. Only quarterbacks, point guards, or school presidents—guys her dead father would have heartily approved of—had been worth her notice. Looking back now at her high school and college years through an adult lens, she saw her actions a tad differently. How had Eric viewed her rejection? Subtlety hadn't been one of her virtues back then either.

Oh, heavens. Her face quickly heated at the memory of a stuck-up princess who thought she was better than him.

Well, she'd certainly gotten her comeuppance. Her father would have loved Blaine. On paper, he was everything Joshua ever wanted for his daughter. Polished, a go-getter, smart, funny. The president of his fraternity. No wonder Simone had had stars in her eyes where Blaine was concerned. If she'd looked closer, she'd have seen the discrepancies in time to avoid him. He was also cruel, conniving, and deceitful.

Last night, she'd spent a couple of hours scouring the Internet for information about him and his family. God help her, he was running for senator in the state of Maryland. His brother was a US congressman, and his father, a recently retired US senator, had served two terms after she'd left the area.

Simone had known of his family's interest in politics. But the fact that Moorecroft Senior would have been eyeing a senate seat when his son was in college gave her a more intimate look at their motivation for wanting to keep everything hush-hush. Still despicable, their threats seemed more understandable now.

The apple never fell far from the tree. If Blaine was guilty of raping her, there was no telling what his father would do if he thought his dynasty could come tumbling down with the truth about Amelia—a granddaughter who wasn't supposed to live.

And Lorraine knew nothing about what happened. Simone hadn't wanted to disrupt her mother's newfound happiness with such ugliness, so she'd run to Georgia and had her baby on her own.

Steering the topic away from Blaine, she asked, "Do you miss Daddy?"

Her mother stopped pouring and sighed heavily. "Yes. Every day of my life. Even when I was married to Dean. Your father and I were soul mates." Then she looked around and sighed again, this one softer. "Don't misunderstand. I loved Dean and cherished the time we had together before he died; but it was a different kind of love. I've been lucky to have two wonderful men in my life. I mourned both husbands, but I'd never regret marrying either one."

"That's beautiful, Momma." How wonderful would it be to trust someone enough to fall in love, not once, but twice, like her mother had?

Lorraine reached out to tuck a stray hair behind her daughter's ear and then patted her face, much like Simone had done to Amelia earlier. That it was something she'd obviously picked up from her mom filled her with contentment.

"I was still a bitch."

"You were young and grieving. What matters most is how you are now." Lorraine shot her a glance. "I'm still curious as to what brought this on."

"Eric Coleman."

"Eric Coleman? That name sounds familiar." Lorraine finished pouring, then set the three glasses on the tray and added cheese, chips, and two dips. "Now I remember the name. He was such a nice boy."

"He lives in my complex. I barely remembered him."

"Oh, honey. He used to pass by our house on his way home from school. He'd always wave to you. I even invited him in for cookies and milk a couple of times."

"He said he asked me out and I broke his heart. That makes me sound like a bitch." She didn't add that just last night, she'd acted like one again. Maybe it was the man who brought it out in her. But that didn't make sense if her mom thought he was a "nice boy." Lorraine Morgan was a good judge of character.

Remorse settled in Simone's stomach at the memory of his backhanded wave after her belated admission that she remembered him.

"Darn," she whispered. Her faulty memory had definitely hurt his feelings. She hadn't wanted to be rude during their earlier meeting either. Yet, after seeing how two men, total strangers, had gained Amelia's trust so easily, she hadn't known what else to do.

Simone sighed. "I think I treated him poorly."

"You think?"

"Okay, I did treat him poorly." Then and now. "He didn't fit my profile of the perfect man."

"The perfect man?"

Geez, what was with her mom and the repeated questions? As soon as the thought was out, she realized what irritated her wasn't the questions but the truth about her behavior and having to admit to being cruel.

"Yes. I had a list of things that reminded me of Dad. If a guy didn't measure up, then I didn't date him."

"What kind of list?"

"Oh, you know—" Simone was saved from having to elaborate when the screen door burst open and Amelia ran in with the kitten in tow.

"I'm thirsty. I thought you were getting lemonade."

"I was, sweetheart." Lorraine put down a small bowl of water. "I bet Buttons would like a drink." Grabbing the full tray, she smiled and said, "Happy hour has officially started."

Amelia's laugh escaped and she glanced at Simone. "This is fun, Mom. I'm so glad you decided to live close to Grandma. I love it here." Then she wrapped her arms around Simone and squeezed.

Simone hugged her fiercely. "I love it too."

Her daughter leaned back and said in a conspiratorial voice, "I'm glad you have a boyfriend to go out with."

She ruffled Amelia's hair and grinned. "Me too." But it wasn't Michael Belk she thought of as the boyfriend she wanted to go out with. It was Eric Coleman.

And for the life of her, she wasn't sure what to do with the revelation.

CHAPTER EIGHT

J UST AFTER they finished dinner that evening, Simone was startled when the doorbell rang. She stared through the peephole, surprised to see Eric standing on the other side of the door. The man was all she could think about since Amelia's comment about a boyfriend. Had her thoughts conjured him up?

Now would be the perfect time to apologize, for yesterday and for high school.

"Hi." Smiling, she opened the door wide. "Come on in."

Eric blinked, his guarded expression practically shouting his reluctance to step over the threshold.

"Okay." He cleared his throat and tugged at his shirt collar. "Thanks. I think."

When he hesitated further, she grabbed his hand and said playfully, "I won't bite. I promise."

"What if I like women who bite?"

She halted in mid-step and turned back to him. Noting the twinkle in his eyes, she grinned. Then she sobered and remembered her purpose. Suddenly tongue-tied, she pursed her lips, shoved her hands into her pockets, and glanced up at him.

After swallowing the mountain-sized lump of embarrassment that had formed in the back of her throat, she was able to choke out, "I was a fool for turning you down in such a rude way in high school, and I'm very sorry." She looked down at the floor, too ashamed to keep meeting such a warm gaze. "And I'm sorry about yesterday too."

"Apology accepted. Would you like to seal it with a kiss?"

"Umm . . . umm . . ." On her third "um," he laughed and closed the door behind them.

"Now that we've totally embarrassed each other, I'll get to the reason for my visit."

Lordy, he had gorgeous brown eyes, made more soulful with his long lashes and coal-black eyebrows. And dimples. Who had dimples these days? He could easily pass for a younger Tom Selleck, except Eric was hotter. Sexier.

Simone had the urge to run her fingers through that wavy, thick black mane of his to see if it was as soft as it looked. *Good grief.* Eric just said something, and being too engrossed in assessing him, she had no clue what.

As flames of heat warmed her cheeks, she licked her lips. "Could you repeat that?"

"I asked where Amelia was."

"Amelia?"

"Your daughter?

"Of course she's my daughter." Funny, she couldn't ever remember forgetting about Amelia before now. Well, not that she really had, but her mind had gone blank for way too long. "Amelia's in her room. Would you like to talk to her?"

"I really came to talk to you."

"Me?"

"Yes, you." He eyed her curiously. "Is that a problem?"

"Oh, no." To keep from looking like a total idiot in front of him, she led him into her living room and indicated the sofa with her hand. "Have a seat. Would you like something to drink?" She pressed her lips together, not sure why she suddenly felt so nervous around him. "I have soft drinks, iced tea, or beer."

"Iced tea would be great."

Instead of sitting, he followed her into the kitchen and stood in the doorway. She felt his gaze on her back as she retrieved a pitcher of tea from the fridge and poured him a tall glass. Her steady hands surprised her, considering the explosions of excitement firing in her midsection. An odd sensation, to be sure. This whole attraction for someone of the opposite sex was as unfamiliar as was the desire to find out more about him. It has been a long, long time since she'd felt this kind of a tug toward a man.

Simone handed Eric a full glass. Her fingers brushed his, and the contact was electric. Definitely shocking. She chanced a quick peek at him. His focus was zeroed in on hers. For a second, his gaze was hot enough to start a forest fire. Then the look was gone. Simone wasn't sure if she'd imagined it out of wishful thinking or not.

Had to be wishful thinking. Eric was clearly not the type to give a woman a second chance to turn him down cold.

"I like your place."

His voice drew her gaze.

She watched him sit, then took a seat across from him. "I like it too, but it's not mine. I subleased it from a couple who are in Europe for a year."

Eric nodded, and the silence between them stretched.

Finally, Simone asked, "What did you want to talk to me about that concerns my daughter?"

"Amelia asked me for Scotty's phone number." He put up a hand when she started to object. "Just hear me out before you go all *helicopter mom* on me."

Simone sat back and crossed her arms. Eyeing him warily, she gave him a curt nod. "Go on."

He spent a moment explaining about Scotty's offer, Amelia's boredom, and her mention of tennis camp. "I think she's afraid she won't be competitive with the other kids."

Simone had no clue that was how Amelia felt. "Due to circumstances beyond her control, she hasn't practiced much lately, but she's really good." Obviously, her daughter was hiding a few insecurities.

"She'll gain more confidence playing against Scotty. And practice makes perfect. Scotty's even willing to drop his usual tennis partners for the opportunity to show her a few things. He'll work on your schedule, mornings or evenings. Whatever you prefer."

A trickle of guilt rose up as Simone eyed her iced tea. Amelia had complained of being bored. As a few drops of condensation ran down the outside of the glass, Simone's mind spun.

Abruptly uprooted from her friends in Georgia, Amelia hadn't had an opportunity to make new ones yet. Buttons would keep her attention for another day or so, but then she'd be bored again until she went off to camp. It seemed like a win-win situation.

"Are you sure he wouldn't mind?"

As well as looking up Blaine online, she'd googled Eric. He was a partner with two other guys. Scotty was the director of information technology at the same company.

"Are you kidding? Working with a kid as talented as Amelia is like a dream come true for him. He'll live vicariously through her achievements." Eric smiled, those sexy dimples making her mind go blank for a nanosecond. "He wanted to go pro, but ended up at MIT instead. Go figure." He paused a moment. "Amelia told me someone tried to kidnap her. Is that true?"

If only her daughter hadn't mentioned the ordeal. Simone worried the inside of her cheek and inhaled deeply, wishing she could forget that day. Finally, she nodded. "It was horrible, and why I moved back home."

"You won't have to worry about her while we're around."

As strange as it seemed, his promise comforted her. "I don't know what to say, except yes." Things were falling into place for them. Simone offered him a genuine smile. "Mornings would work better. I worry about her being alone so much. She has no friends, since school hasn't started yet." What could it hurt? They'd be outside and Amelia would love it.

"Great." Eric stood. Shoving his hands into his pockets, he turned to her. "I'll talk with Scotty and set something up, then get back to you. You can give the good news to Amelia."

"Sounds like a plan." Simone jumped up to escort him out since he seemed ready to leave.

As they walked side by side toward the door, Eric added, "My partner has a kid about Amelia's age. We should all get together."

"That would be nice."

"Nice? That word is like the kiss of death to a guy."

A devil-may-care grin was back, along with those dimples. That alone sent her heart rate soaring, but when accompanied with his teasing tone, she had a hard time restraining herself from wanting to do something that wasn't nice—which was so unlike her.

"Is fun a better word choice?" she asked as they exchanged numbers.

He nodded. "Much." At the same time, his eyes zeroed in on her lips. "I'd like to spend more time with you."

The sound of his voice was pure honey, sweet and flowing. Goosebumps trailed up her arms in response. Her reaction to him should have concerned her. The fact that it didn't, however, *did* concern her.

Eric Coleman was dangerous. He'd proven it by having an uncanny ability to slide underneath the solid wall she'd erected around herself. He definitely had perfected the technique of throwing her off guard.

What would he think if he knew how Amelia was conceived? She never dwelled on the subject because she'd never met anyone she cared enough about to reveal the specifics. Until now. She shook away the thoughts as silly.

"Are you sure about that?"

"You forget. I was half in love with you. Just like every guy in the senior class."

"Yes, and I turned you down. Remember?" She opened the door to hurry him out. Not because she was afraid of him, but because she was more afraid of herself. "Good night, Eric."

He stepped outside.

About to shut the door, she halted when he spun back around. A second later, he was in her space, reaching for her shoulders. Shocked, she stood immobile and watched him lower his head. His grip on her shoulders relaxed, giving her plenty of opportunity to step out of his grasp or turn her head away.

Simone did neither. Instead she relished the rush of excitement that enveloped her as his lips covered hers.

For long seconds, he kissed her as if he were a seed in the desert needing water to sprout and she were a spring rain. Or maybe it was her kissing him that way? It didn't seem to matter. The kiss slaked both their thirsts.

Simone felt a sense of loss when his mouth left hers, but it was short lived. His lips blazed a trail along her jaw and her neck to her ear.

"I've always wondered what you'd taste like," Eric whispered. He spent seconds nibbling there before his soft mouth found its way back to her lips, grazing once, twice, three times. "Now I know."

She moaned in appreciation. The featherlight kisses had her insides burning for more. Disappointment filled her when he broke away.

Pressing his forehead against hers, he said, "I did love you, you know."

When she finally opened her eyes, he was halfway down the walkway.

Simone closed the door, stunned at the sense of loneliness that ate at her with Eric's departure. For the first time in her adult life, Amelia wasn't enough to fill the void in her heart.

"STUPID. STUPID. Stupid," Eric mumbled as he inserted the key to unlock his front door. Now inside, he leaned against the cool wood, struggling to understand why he'd actually done something so inane as to kiss Simone. Worse, he'd admitted to loving her. Her, of all women?

His confession and the way he'd swooped in and kissed her had clearly shocked her. Hell, he'd stunned himself. Under normal circumstances, he'd have a drink to wipe away the memory. Only this time, he wanted to remember everything about those few seconds.

Recalling the promise he'd made about connecting with his friends, he brought up Sin's number on his cell phone and pressed SEND.

Sin answered on the second ring. "Yeah, Eric. What's up?"

"I need a favor that involves having me, a friend, and her daughter, who's Andy's age, to dinner at your place. I was hoping for this Friday, since the daughter is going off to camp on

Saturday."

"Sure thing. I'll tell Avery. We can barbecue."

Eric smiled. No questions—just an agreement, which was so like Sin.

They discussed who'd bring what and set a time before Eric said his good-byes and disconnected the call. He then sent a text off to Simone.

Her quick acceptance had the wheels of anticipation churning inside his gut. The burning desire to spend more time with her should bother him, considering their past. It didn't. What bothered him more was the idea that Friday night was four days too many to wait.

He'd just have to make a pest of himself in the meantime.

CHAPTER NINE

TUESDAY MORNING, Amelia waited in front of Eric's car while bouncing a tennis ball on her racket. Forty-five bounces later, Eric strode up just as Scotty drove into the lot and parked in a visitor's space.

She caught the ball and grinned. "Thanks for talking to my mom."

"No problem." Eric hit his keyless entry. The cool lights on his sporty car flashed and the locks clicked open.

Scotty ambled toward them, swinging his racket, and Amelia refocused on Eric as he climbed inside his car. "She's been nutso over letting me do anything this summer because of what happened."

"Yeah, I heard."

"Heard what?" Scotty came to stand next to her, his expression curious. "What happened?"

Amelia shrugged, resisting the urge to roll her eyes. "At my old school, somebody tried to kidnap me."

"You're kidding!"

"It's old news, Scotty." Eric shut his door, and the engine roared to life. "See you two later."

As he drove away, Amelia stared after the car, thankful he'd sprung her from prison for a few hours every morning. She glanced at Scotty. "Are you ready to get whipped?"

Holding up a hand to block out the bright sunlight, he squinted and grunted. "In your dreams. But first things first. Spill your guts, kid."

"I'd rather play tennis than talk. It happened so fast, and it was over a month ago. I don't really remember much."

Scotty crossed his arms. "I'm not budging until my curiosity is satisfied."

Glaring at him, she put her hands on her hips and said a little too loudly, "Someone tried to kidnap me." She stomped toward the courts. "Now can we play?"

"Wait." Scotty caught up with her. "You can't drop a bombshell like that and then just walk away."

"I'd rather forget about it." She certainly didn't want to talk about it. But since he seemed genuinely interested and was helping her out, she let out a sigh and shrugged. "There's not much to tell. It happened during lunch. Just some weird guy trying to steal a kid from the school playground."

Scotty's low whistle matched his surprised expression. "No wonder your mom was upset when we first met her. If somebody tried to kidnap my daughter, I'd be on guard until she graduated from college."

Amelia lost the struggle to keep from rolling her eyes. "I guess it's lucky I'm not your kid, then." Done talking about it, she started for the courts.

Scotty must have gotten the message because he followed her without another word. She hurried over to her side of the court and leaned forward, facing him, bouncing back and forth on the balls of her feet as she waited for his serve. When it came rocketing over the net, spinning with a bit of English, it was obvious Scotty wasn't going to take it easy on her today.

Amelia didn't mind. With the beginning of tennis camp less than a week away, she relished the opportunity to sharpen her game. Grinning, she dove for the shot and sent it back Scotty's way with a vicious backhand that blasted the neon-yellow ball straight at his chest.

Eat that!

<><><>

SIMONE SMILED as Michael held out her chair and waited for her to sit. The restaurant was crowded, and they were lucky to find an empty table.

"Thanks." She picked up her menu. Few guys bothered with the gentlemanly habit in this day and age. Not that she was any expert on the way men acted during lunch dates, considering her last date, lunch or otherwise, had been in college. No matter, the small gesture made her feel special. It also had an amazing effect on her opinion of Michael, erasing the usual wariness she clung to when around any man.

Simone was bound and determined to get over her fear of men. Last night with Eric had proven she wanted to be normal. She wanted to be a strong, confident woman when she was with him, at ease in her own skin and comfortable enough to be sexy, not wary and gun-shy like a panic-stricken sexual-assault survivor. Having normal dates with guys like Michael gave her the opportunity to practice her dating skills, which furthered her plan.

"Did I say something to upset you?"

Pulled from her thoughts, she shook her head. "No. Why do you ask?"

"You seemed a million miles away."

The waiter strode up, interrupting what could have been an awkward moment. Instead, Simone smiled and shrugged off Michael's concern. "I was deciding what to order." She turned to the waiter and ordered a turkey sandwich and soup, thanking her lucky stars that she'd had that very same thing a few days ago and knew it was on the menu.

After that, Simone tried to be as cordial and personable as she could. Not as easy task, considering opening up wasn't something she enjoyed. Still, she kept to the basics and spoke in generalities.

"Where'd you go to school?" she asked after a short lull in the conversation.

"High school or college?"

He really had an engaging smile, Simone decided. "College."

As Michael opened up about his life, more of her reticence

toward him eased. He really was a nice guy. Too bad she'd become fascinated with Eric. Who knew what might have happened otherwise?

Don't be stupid, her common sense shouted. *Eric is past history.* Considering her treatment of him back in high school, she didn't see how he'd give her another chance to reject him, no matter that the air practically sizzled when he was around.

The waiter returned with their meals and refilled their glasses. As Simone picked up her sandwich and took a bite, she mulled over her predicament. She really should just forget Eric and concentrate on Michael. After all, he was in the here and now, and they were starting with a clean slate, no embarrassing baggage from the past to hamper them.

Heavens, her life was much less complicated when she lived in Georgia.

When Michael made a comment about comparing her job in Norcross to her job in DC, Simone didn't think too much about it. After all, they'd been swapping information.

Yet when Michael said something about her daughter, she glanced up at him. "How did you know I have a daughter?"

His eyes narrowed and sharpened with a hardness but was gone so quickly, Simone questioned whether her mind was playing tricks on her. For some reason, Michael made her nervous, like he wasn't what he appeared to be. Or maybe she was looking for some reason to boot him out of her life so she could focus her efforts back on Eric. Geez, she was being pathetic now.

That engaging smile came back, creating laugh lines around his eyes and softening the hawkish stare that his glasses had magnified only a second ago. "You mentioned her yesterday."

Simone smiled, remembering the offhand comment. "So I did." Her paranoia was back, annoying her since she'd made a conscious effort to leave all her worry back in Georgia. After all, she had made a careless mistake, something she regretted now.

"How long have you been in DC?" she asked, changing the subject.

Amelia was off-limits to any prospective suitor until Simone felt comfortable enough for introductions. Eric and Scotty were exceptions since her daughter had already met them. Unfortunately, that might never happen with Michael. The realization was proof enough that they would never go further than lunch dates.

LATER AT work, Simone contemplated her situation. Michael might not be someone she was interested in, but he'd helped her figure out that she wanted more out of life. Eric and his sexy smile came to mind, as did their shared kiss. Her insides tingled just from the anticipation of a repeat performance.

The more she thought about it, the more she recognized a need to work on changing Eric's opinion of her. After all, he was the man who fascinated her—not Michael. Michael might be nice and pleasant, but Eric evoked sensations in her that she hadn't felt in years, feelings she realized she wanted to explore.

A dinner invitation popped into her head. Simone wasn't the best cook, but she could scrounge up something. Amelia liked Eric and he liked her daughter, so she'd use that to her advantage.

At the end of the day, on the way to her mother's house to pick up Amelia, Simone glanced in the rearview mirror and spotted a black pickup lagging a few cars behind.

Was he following her? She couldn't be sure. Instead of making her usual turn onto her mother's street, she passed it and made the next right, then drove around the block. At each turn, her gaze remained fastened on the mirror. She heaved a sigh of relief when no one followed her.

Still, the incident scared the bejeebers out of her. She'd become too complacent, and that was about to change.

After parking and exiting the car, she clicked the keyless lock with a shaky hand. She hurried up the walk, determined to be more diligent about watching her back.

Inside, Amelia's laughter caught Simone's attention and she shook off her trepidation. Her daughter didn't need to know how frightened she'd been.

Pasting a smile on her face, she headed for the back deck. At the screen door, which was open to let in the cool afternoon breeze, she stood for a moment, watching her daughter.

Amelia was on her back and the kitten was batting at her hair. "You're so cute." Her daughter snuggled the cat between her chin and shoulder. "I wish I could take you with me to camp."

"I doubt Buttons would do well at camp. She can't play tennis," Lorraine said, drawing more of Amelia's laughter.

It did Simone's heart good to see Amelia so happy. Too bad there hadn't been a lot of that until recently. She must have made a noise because her mother glanced in her direction.

"You're just in time, Simone." Lorraine stood. "We were going to have popsicles."

Amelia jumped up. "Mom," she said, hugging her. "I had the best day. I loved playing tennis with Scotty. He taught me a few tricks."

The three headed back inside toward the kitchen with Amelia talking a mile a minute about her *awesome* practice.

"What do you think about inviting Scotty and Eric to dinner tonight?" Simone shrugged, keeping her expression neutral. "You know, to thank them?"

"Cool. And I can play another set with Scotty afterward." Amelia skipped to the chair where her backpack lay.

That was one way of getting some alone time with Eric. Simone didn't articulate the thought, but said instead, "We'll have to call and see if they can come. It's spur of the moment, after all."

"Don't worry. Scotty said he'd be happy to play more if I wanted."

As Lorraine opened the freezer and pulled out a few popsicles, Amelia reached for her cell phone. "I'll text Scotty right now."

"I'll ask Eric." While Amelia was texting, Simone decided a text was the perfect way to approach him. That way, she wouldn't seem overly anxious. Seconds after she sent the message, she got his response.

Eric: Would love to. What time?

Simone: How about 7:30?

Eric: Sounds great. What should I bring?

Simone: Just yourself.

As she stuck her phone back into her purse, Amelia shouted, "Scotty's in."

"Great. So's Eric."

Lorraine picked up the tray she'd loaded. "I'm so glad you've found some friends."

"They're nice." Simone gave a little shrug, trying to act as if a thousand butterflies hadn't taken flight inside her belly.

She mentally rubbed her hands together. Her impromptu dinner invite just might yield some results. She felt safe with her neighbor and his friend. If that black pickup happened to show up again, nothing would happen with those two near.

<><><>

HE DIDN'T risk driving to the grandmother's house. Instead he parked in an obscure space near the condos and waited until he spotted Simone's Beetle leave. He checked his watch and smiled smugly before putting the car into gear and driving away.

Right on time.

He'd be back tomorrow. His hands on the steering wheel itched to take action.

Soon. Soon both would be dead. Then he could move on to his next project.

CHAPTER TEN

THE DOORBELL chimed. With a bottle of wine in hand, Eric hurried to open the door. "For once you're on time, good buddy."

"I'm never late when someone offers to feed me." Scotty's nod indicated the wine. "I see you're trying to gain favor with the mom?"

"Her name's Simone, and I don't see how bringing a bottle of wine to dinner is anything more than being polite."

"A might touchy, aren't we?"

Glancing at Scotty, Eric hid all emotion under a blank stare.

"Nice try. You're sweet on the lady. And I'm here to do you a favor."

Eric lifted his brows, still maintaining his neutral expression. "Oh?"

Scotty clapped him on the back. "Amelia and I are going to play a set after we eat, which should give you two some one-on-one time."

"Thanks." Eric eyed him cautiously. "I think."

In silence, they made the trip up the stairs to Simone's third-floor condo. Thank God, Scotty decided not to give him any more grief about Simone and his infatuation with her.

As it was, Eric had a hard enough time keeping his emotions in check when it came to the lady in question. Excitement had built to an unprecedented level in the time between Simone's text and now. He couldn't wait to see her, and the great thing about the invitation was that she'd initiated it. Hopefully that meant she was interested in him.

Simone opened the door right as Eric was about to knock. Dressed casually in shorts and a summery blue top that brought out her eyes, she offered them a wide smile.

"Glad you could make it on such short notice."

"Are you kidding? I'll never pass up a home-cooked meal," Scotty said, pushing his way past Eric and thankfully covering his hesitation at responding. Simone stole his breath and left him tongue-tied.

"I wasn't sure if I should bring white or red," he was finally able to croak out. It was as if he'd reverted to that undeserving kid in high school, trapped in a world where she was out of reach.

"Red's fine. Thanks." She relieved him of the wine and held the door open while stepping aside.

Eric followed Scotty inside, stuffing his unease behind his usual smile. It was such a stupid way to feel after all this time. He thought he was over being that unloved kid. He'd become somebody in the ensuing years. Nevertheless, his father's verbal lashings about being worthless continued to worm their way into his psyche. And the simple truth did nothing to expel them.

Would he ever be normal enough to meet a woman like Simone at her level?

"Would you like a glass before dinner?" Simone glanced first at Eric, then at Scotty.

"Sure," Eric said.

But Scotty shook his head, saying, "None for me. I need a clear head when I play against Amelia after dinner.

"Darn it," Amelia said, appearing in the doorway leading to the hall. "I was hoping you'd have at least one glass so I'd have a slight edge."

Scotty chuckled. "Dream on, sweetcakes. Prepare to meet your doom."

Tuning out the friendly banter about who was the better player, Eric noted the graceful way Simone uncorked the bottle. He kept his gaze on her as she poured two glasses and then offered him one.

"Here's to friendship." She held up her glass.

Eric's gaze stayed fastened on hers as he took a sip. The glint of awareness in her eyes offered more than mere friendship, but he chalked that up to one fact. She viewed him as eye candy, the same as those girls in high school who helped him pass his courses.

He shoved the thought aside, unwilling to let the past screw up the present. Or the future. If there was one with Simone.

"Is there anything I can do to help with dinner?" He sniffed the air. "Smells wonderful." His stomach growled in agreement. "Sorry. I didn't have lunch," he said when she laughed.

The sweet sound of her soft laughter zinged all the way from his ears to his groin. "So I'm hungrier than usual," he added. It would be rude to add that he was hungry for more than food.

Damn! He had to get his mind out of the gutter or he'd never survive the next few hours without her thinking he was a horndog.

"Come on. I'll put you to work," Simone said as she headed for the kitchen.

Eric followed, happy to have a distraction. She deserved to be wooed, and that's just what he planned to do, despite that inner voice telling him she could do better.

<><><>

SIMONE HAD ample time during the meal to surreptitiously scope out Eric as everyone discussed Amelia's upcoming tennis camp.

Surprisingly, Amelia had become quite the chatterbox with Scotty. It was clear that she loved the idea of besting the man on the courts. After only one morning of playing tennis with him, she'd lost the fear of not being good enough.

In turn, Scotty talked about computers. Then he and Amelia got into a conversation about the latest game taking over the Internet.

"That's awesome. I've only gotten to level ten," Amelia said when Scotty mentioned making it all the way through to the Chamber of Death. "You'll have to give me some pointers."

Other than when she was playing with Buttons, her daughter's expression was the most animated Simone had noted since moving home.

"I'd rather play tennis." Scotty wiped his mouth with a napkin and set it beside his empty plate.

"Well, duh. So would I, but after that, I'd love to figure out how to bust into the Creeping Jungle. Unless it's a secret, and if you tell me you'll have to kill me."

Scotty laughed, then turned to Simone. "That was the best meal I've had in ages. Thanks for inviting me."

"You're welcome. I wanted to do something to reciprocate." Simone smiled. "Amelia's having the time of her life."

Just watching how Scotty and Eric brought her daughter out made her realize that, while she'd tried to be both mother and father for Amelia, men were important role models for girls. Another reason for Simone to keep these men around for a while and stay her course with Eric. How sad that she hadn't been interested in what effect a positive male influence could have on their lives before now.

Simone pushed away from the table. If she'd chosen Eric all those years ago, her past would be completely rewritten, and her faith in men wouldn't have been shattered. On the other hand, she wouldn't have Amelia.

"Go ahead and get out to the courts. Dishes can wait."

"Thanks, Mom." Amelia hugged her, then rushed to grab her racket.

Scotty and Eric stood at the same time.

"I'll help you do dishes while they play." Eric reached for Scotty's plate.

"Thanks for the offer, but that can wait."

"I insist. After all, you cooked a wonderful meal. If anything, I'm hoping my cleaning-up services will earn me a repeat invitation."

How could she refuse his warm gaze, especially when accompanied by those dimples. Both twisted her insides into one tight knot. "I wouldn't want to disappoint you."

In silent companionship, they cleared the table, working

together like they'd been doing it for years instead of just having been reacquainted a few days ago.

"You rinse." Simone pointed to the sink. "And I'll load the dishwasher, since I have a system."

"Ah."

Glancing at him, she narrowed her eyes. "What does that mean?"

Eric grinned. "I should have known you'd have a system. Women always do."

"Is that right?" Simone couldn't keep a straight face, not when his eyes held such good humor. "So you're saying I'm predictable."

"Now there you're wrong. You're not at all what I expected." Eric rinsed a plate and handed it to her. His expression sobered. "You're much nicer. Softer," he whispered.

Tingles of excitement rose up her spine at the flirtatious tone in his voice. Simone had forgotten how enjoyable it was to find someone of the opposite sex attractive; how nice it was to want to flirt. Unfortunately, she was like an Eskimo in the Amazon rainforest when it came to knowing how to respond.

Rather than rely on pretense, she answered honestly. "I'm glad. I hate the thought of being considered a bitch."

His brow furrowed and he shook his head. "I never considered you one."

"Oh?" That was a surprise.

"I took it to mean you were choosy. And rightfully so, considering I came from the wrong side of the tracks."

"That's even worse." She frowned. "I'd rather have you think me a bitch than a snob."

"Trust me." He went back to rinsing the plate in his hand before handing it to her. "Neither description crossed my mind."

Gripping the dripping plate he offered, she shot him a quick glance. "Then what did you think?"

He laughed, but the warm humor she'd heard earlier in his voice had completely disappeared. "I was a lowlife. Why would someone like you consider dating someone like me?"

She bristled. "That's absurd."

"It's true. I had nothing to offer."

"What?" Unable to keep the surprise off her face, she stared at him openmouthed. "You're an interesting person and someone I'd like to get to know better. You had to have some redeeming qualities to become that person."

"I never thought of it like that."

Simone offered him a self-deprecating smile. "I shouldn't have rushed to judgment back then. Just look at how far you've come without all the advantages I've had. That's impressive."

Her cheeks grew hot as more guilt filled her over how quickly she'd turned him down back then. It didn't matter that she'd been young and naive. Her dismissal had still been obnoxious and rude, and she saw that clearly now.

Glancing at him from beneath her lashes, she said, "I'm surprised you're even talking to me."

Eric grunted. "Obviously we've both learned something from the experience."

"What did you learn?"

He tossed out a derisive laugh and handed her a glass. "It doesn't matter." As she placed it in the dishwasher, he added, "I'm just glad that we've reconnected."

"So am I."

The conversation died as if a MUTE button had been pressed. After placing the last dish in its spot, Simone wiped her hands on the towel and hung it up, searching for something to say.

Now what? The silence became deafening.

She gave Eric a nervous glance. "Would you like another glass of wine?" She reached for the bottle. "That will finish off the wine you brought. If we want more, I can open another."

"I'd love nothing better. That way we'll have more time to get to know each other."

With a shaky hand, Simone poured two glasses, praying her nervousness didn't show.

Eric stepped closer to take the glass she offered. Their hands brushed in the process, and her heart rate soared.

The rush of excitement at being this close to him was hard enough to endure, but every time he glanced her way, those soul-searching eyes connected with her in a way no man ever had. His smile conjured up thoughts of doing naughty things to those dimples. A surprising and unusual realization, to be sure.

"Shall we sit?" She did just that and patted the seat on the sofa next to her.

For the next hour, they did nothing but talk about anything and everything, which was also so unlike Simone. She'd never been this open with anyone.

One thing she discovered as they chatted—Eric was a good listener. Unlike her earlier lunch date with Michael, there had been no reticence to overcome, and the words just flowed from her mouth.

The wine helped, of course, but it was more the man.

Simone's attraction for Eric grew. The more she was with him, the more she wanted to be with him. More importantly, she trusted him. Her father would have liked him. She said as much, which led to talking about her dad.

"You're lucky to have known such a wonderful man," Eric said when she mentioned how hard it had been getting over his death.

"I just wish I'd had him longer. What about you?" She tossed a handful of hair behind her shoulder, feeling slightly embarrassed. "I've been chatting your ear off and haven't given you a chance to get a word in. What about your family?"

"It's better if I leave them out of the conversation."

"That bad?"

"Worse. They didn't give me the best start. But I had Sin. And we had a couple of cops for mentors."

"Sin?"

"Jeff Sinclair. The partner I told you about, the one who's having the barbecue. In fact, Avery, his wife, is making it a party. She invited her mother; her sister, Terry; and Terry's husband, Des—he's our other partner, and Des's mom. You should ask your mom. The more, the merrier."

"I'm sure my mom would love the chance to meet my new friends." She had no idea why she felt so comfortable opening up; she just knew that Eric would never use the information to hurt her.

"What can I bring?"

Then it dawned on her. Eric didn't strike her as someone who lied. Unlike Blaine Moorecroft. Even Michael Belk seemed to be hiding something, which meant he could also be lying. Had her sixth sense recognized something in Michael that reminded her of Blaine? Or did she just enjoy talking to Eric, and as a result, let her guard down? She pushed the disturbing thoughts away for further reflection later.

Much later.

"I'll find out if there's anything you can bring." Eric's voice pulled her back to the conversation about the barbecue. "And let you know."

She nodded. "Thanks."

He flashed those incredible dimples again, and the look in his eyes as their gazes met had her insides doing somersaults.

"That's settled, so what do we do now?" The playful flirtatious tone in his voice sent her stomach tumbling further.

Unable to let this opportunity to flirt slip by, she picked up her wine. Eyeing him over the rim, she took a drink. "I'd like to know more about you." Feeling a bit bolder, she gave him a big smile and laid her cards on the table. "Since we both seem interested."

"I'm definitely interested."

"Good to know I'm not the only one."

Damn, but it was hard not to wonder what sleeping with him would be like when he looked at her with that intense gaze, as he was doing right now. And wasn't that an interesting twist? Her thinking about sex. With a man. Simone barely recognized herself.

"Well?" he said after another pause, motioning for her to go on.

She cleared her throat, feeling heat spread up her face. Had he read her mind? Lord, Eric Coleman might just be out of her league. Ha! She was still in Little League compared to his Major League status.

Eric held his palms out. "I'm an open book, so ask me anything about my past."

Her gaze narrowed. "Anything?"

He nodded, appearing totally relaxed when her stomach was knotted so tight, it took every ounce of energy she could muster to act as if she did this kind of thing all the time.

How on earth could she flirt with him and not come out unsinged?

There was only one way to find out.

When she felt confident enough to speak without giving more of her thoughts away, she said, "We'll start with the basics. Okay?" She glanced at him with eyebrows cocked. "After high school, what did you do? Go to college? Work?" Thankfully, the questions flowed and her self-confidence returned.

"I wanted to do the whole college thing with my friends but had limited funds, and I didn't like the thought of going into debt. I got a couple of years at a community college while in the Air Force." After spending a few minutes giving her a rundown on his life since leaving the Air Force, which included the work he now did for SPC Electronics as director of sales, he gave her a wry grin. "How about you? I imagine you were in a sorority and all that?"

"I was for the first year. Until I got pregnant."

Not the flirtiest of topics, but it seemed important to bring up. Simone was surprised that she was able to speak about the memory without emotion overwhelming her. Maybe talking about it did ease the pain she'd always buried over the incident. She'd never spoken openly about that time to anyone.

Wanting to keep the conversation light, she shrugged. "Then I changed schools and majors. With a baby on the way, fun and games didn't suit me any longer."

"What about Amelia's father?" Eric asked after a short lull in the conversation. "Where's he?"

Simone pursed her lips.

"I'm sorry. That's obviously too personal a subject."

"I should be over it by now. He's history."

"As in not dead?" His lips curled into a sheepish smile. "When I first saw you, I thought maybe you were a widow."

"No. He's very much alive." A fact that had hit her square in the face a week ago. Staring at a point on the floor, she brought her thumb to her mouth and nibbled on her nail. Then she shrugged and smiled wanly. "I met him during rush week my first year in college. Thought he was like my dad, but that didn't turn out to be the case."

"Ah." A knowing expression crossed Eric's face. "Does he see Amelia?"

"No." Averting her gaze, she picked a piece of lint off her shorts. Finally, she looked up. "He and his family urged me to get an abortion and waived all rights when they paid me off."

"Whoa. That's . . ." He swiped a hand over his face and blew out a sigh. Compassion flared in his eyes. "Shit. I don't know what to say."

"Shitty works to describe him." She gave Eric an abbreviated version of the story, then quickly moved on to the life she'd created in Georgia after leaving town. "As far as I'm concerned, he is dead. That's what I told Amelia. It's better than not being wanted. If she ever finds out the truth, I hope she'll forgive me for lying." Oh boy, this was getting too deep. She definitely needed to work on her flirting skills.

"Trust me, forgiveness is easy when you have a child's best interest at heart. It's understandable. What isn't as forgivable is being unwanted and abused because of it." Eric eyed her curiously. "Could he be behind the kidnapping attempt?"

Simone shook her head. "I seriously doubt it since he didn't want her to begin with."

"What if he's had second thoughts?"

"Then why not contact me directly?" His family had the power to use the law to force their way into Amelia's life. The notion left a hole in her heart. *Over my dead body.*

"What?"

Oops. "Nothing." She smiled at him, holding the fear at bay. "I was just thinking out loud."

What if the Moorecroft family did know about her daughter? Would they have Amelia kidnapped, or worse, try to kill her? The mere thought sent ice water through her veins.

The more she thought about it, the more it didn't make sense. Clifton Moorecroft, Blaine's father, might have the balls to send the guy in the black pickup, but why would he? Simone had never been a threat.

"He wasn't into taking on the responsibility of a child. I doubt he's changed his mind." Although her voice held confidence, doubts swirled.

"So you just let him off the hook?" Eric shrugged when she gave him a sharp look. "You don't have to answer. Just call me super nosy."

Her flirting skills were nosediving. Fast. Still, he did deserve to know some of the sordid truth if they were to go further.

"Not totally. I did receive a hefty amount of financial support. In advance. I didn't push for more. To do so would have meant an ugly uphill battle that I had no desire to fight. Not when his mom and dad couldn't accept that their precious son had actually lowered himself to impregnating a nobody like me."

Of course, raping a nobody like her was another matter entirely, which made it easy for the family to cover it up. Yet it was a little too soon to let Eric in on that tidbit, no matter how sincere and compassionate his expression was.

Simone tried for a warm smile. "We were talking about you, remember?"

Unfortunately, the skepticism in his eyes told her he knew better, but he only nodded.

"You're right. We were talking about me." His demeanor shifted, and he was all charm and smiles once again.

So far Simone was batting zero in the flirting department. Somehow, she had to up her game.

When his gaze lingered on her lips, Simone followed suit, eyeing his lips like she was dying for a taste, which she was. Her cheeks grew hot at the thought.

Lord, you'd think she was a virgin the way her heart was pounding. Of course, she might as well be one, but that fact wouldn't stop her. Not now, when things were just getting interesting.

<><><>

DURING THE last hour, Eric had decided he would much rather listen to Simone talk about her past than share his. She'd definitely had it hard, which made his struggles seem minor. When she asked

77

a direct question about his major in college, he shrugged.

"I got an associate degree in general education through the Air Force. It was a means to an end. I never wanted to grow up to be my father." He snorted. Not even close. "The Air Force gave me structure," he admitted.

Having been so open, she deserved to know more about his past. It didn't hurt that her empathetic expression was a balm against memories that were still an open wound.

"I had a tough time growing up. School never came easy for me."

According to Scotty, it was because of Eric's learning disability. Scotty had even mentioned that most kids with his kind of disability actually had higher IQs, which was why it was hard to pinpoint the kids who struggled with them.

"In high school, girls would help me. It's how I learned to be charming." He made a joke out of it, but charm had little to do with it. Most of those girls who helped him had been in it for the wild ride he could provide, and he'd been horny enough to oblige them.

After two years in the Air Force, Eric had finally realized the implications weren't just him being stupid and immature. Basically, he'd been prostituting himself for their help. Not a pretty memory to have of one's high school years, but that was what it was—pure and simple—a truth that had been hard to stomach.

Somehow Eric didn't think he'd see the same approval in Simone's eyes if he let her in on that deep dark secret. It was probably why he hadn't felt man enough to continue pursuing her after her initial rejection. She deserved so much more than a lowlife like him.

Still, thoughts of kissing her again wouldn't subside, especially after intercepting her signals. He was adept enough to know that they didn't lie.

Thankfully, Amelia and Scotty burst through the front door, saving Eric from having to expand further on his sordid past. Of course, he'd eventually have to divulge the ugliness if they were to have the type of relationship he sought with Simone.

When that time came, Eric hoped he had the courage to be as totally open as she'd been. She deserved total honesty.

CHAPTER ELEVEN

WEDNESDAY NIGHT was basically a repeat of Tuesday night when Eric opened his door to Scotty on his doorstep, racket in hand.

The two had readily agreed to Simone's invite, but Eric had insisted on bringing dessert this time. Balancing the plate of cookies in his right hand, he glanced at the bottle in his left on the way up to her unit. And wine. A good red wine worked wonders for easing nerves. On both sides.

Same as the night before, Amelia greeted them with a wide smile. "Hey, guys. You're just in time. Mom's making one of my favorites."

Grinning, Scotty set his racket down and rubbed his hands together. "I could get used to this. Tennis lessons for home-cooked meals. I'm definitely getting the better end of the bargain."

"Mom doesn't think so, and neither do I." Amelia opened the door wider and said in a conspiratorial tone, "I've improved a lot. Those campers won't know what hit them."

"I'm fresh out of lessons." Eric nodded to his offering covered in clear plastic wrap. "But I did bring my chocolate chip cookies."

"My idea." Scotty shut the door, and as the group veered in the direction of the kitchen, he added, "Trust me, you'll love them." He winked. "You can thank me later."

Eric caught sight of Simone and stopped in mid-step. She'd done something to her hair and was wearing more makeup than usual. Although she was already stunning before the changes, the effect was breathtaking. Unable to speak, he could only stare. The one word that came to mind was *beautiful*, but he had no way of conveying the thought at the moment.

A bit of color hit her cheeks, and she brushed at one of the locks of hair framing her face. "I hope you like lasagna. It's an old family recipe." She reached for two hot pads and opened the oven, sending delicious scents of tomatoes, garlic, and cheese into the air.

Eric finally found his voice. "I'm glad I brought red wine tonight. And as promised," he held up the plate, "cookies. From an old family recipe."

"I could get used to having handsome men plying me with wine and dessert," Simone said with a smile.

Still holding the hot pads, she extracted the glass baking dish from the oven and headed for her dining room, adjacent to the open kitchen. The formal dining table—complete with candles, fine china, and silverware—looked ready for a feast.

The thought that Simone was including the two of them in her family rituals lodged a lump of emotion in Eric's throat. Everything about the meal made him feel special. No woman had ever gone to such trouble for him without expecting sex in return, and he couldn't stop the surge of need from overtaking his system at the thought.

He slanted a quick glance her way and noted her pleased expression. More emotion gripped him deep inside and squeezed. Eric wanted Simone's love now just as much as he had when he was a teen. And looking into her bright blue eyes, he saw a similar need. The realization settled over his shoulders like a warm blanket, heating some of those memories that had kept him emotionally frozen in time.

For the first time in his life—well, not really the first, since he'd felt this way as a teen—he wanted to be a better man. Someone worthy of her. He wasn't sure he was that person, but he was a damn sight better than some frat boy who used her, got her pregnant, and then bought her off.

Amelia laughed. Eric's gaze shifted and he took in the young girl's animated features. If Eric had fathered her, he'd have married Simone on the spot, and would have been proud to claim the girl as his.

The notion added to the all the other realizations he'd come to lately, giving him a clearer view of what love was all about.

This feeling growing inside him wasn't about sex. Of course, Eric wanted to make love to Simone. But therein lay the difference. He wanted to love her and have her love in return. Eric finally understood what *making love* truly meant. It wasn't just about slaking lust and satisfying an urge. It was more about sharing a feeling and getting closer to a person in a way that only sex allowed.

All those other encounters in his past were really empty promises. Encounters that meant nothing and made him feel shallow in hindsight.

Simone shined a different light on the whole process. With her, he could wait. When they made love—damn, he was being optimistic—*if* they happened to make love, Eric would make every effort to ensure that it was something special.

Once his mind started in that direction, Eric couldn't steer clear of thinking of making a life with Simone. Of starting a family. Of sharing home-cooked meals with her and Amelia every night.

Geez, he needed to get a grip. He was getting way ahead of himself. He'd only recently reconnected with her, and already he was planning their wedding and visualizing her pregnant with his baby.

An unfamiliar sense of optimism zipped through him as he took a cheesy bite, eyeing Simone while he chewed. Once he'd swallowed, he smiled in her direction. "Excellent food." Holding her gaze, he picked up his wine and sipped.

Who knew ten years ago that he'd now be sharing dinner with the woman he'd always held in the highest esteem? The turn of events had had an amazing effect on his psyche, negating some of the verbal lashings his father had never seemed to run out of. Those hateful words blared the loudest in his memories, and had affected his outlook from there on out. No matter how much he'd tried to prove his father wrong over the years, he'd always felt he'd fallen short. But maybe with Simone's love, Eric could finally be free of the self-loathing and self-doubt that had always plagued him, even without his father's approval.

Whoa, going pretty deep tonight. Must be the wine and good company. Perhaps these positive surroundings had opened his mind and had him reflecting on dreams and feelings he hadn't even known existed.

One thing about deep thoughts. Once they started, it was like turning on a faucet full blast and not being able to shut it off. And most daunting of all, the revelations pouring out were those Eric hadn't considered before.

Yep. His old man would have a good laugh if he realized that Eric still yearned for the impossible . . . his father's love.

Trish had said their father wanted to see him. Maybe it was time to make peace with the elder Coleman and face Eric's worst fear—that he'd still be nothing in the old man's eyes.

Eric smiled. After being with Simone and experiencing the warmth of her gaze every time he glanced her way during dinner, the fear of that disapproval had diminished to almost nothing.

SIMONE STOOD to begin clearing the table. "Do either of you want a cookie before you head out to the courts?" she asked Amelia and Scotty on her way to the kitchen sink.

"That was the best lasagna I've ever had." Scotty scooted back his chair. "I need to get in a good workout before I can enjoy one of those cookies. Otherwise, I'll get fat."

She grinned. Scotty was what she called slender. He reminded Simone of a younger Woody Allen, not that many people even knew who the actor was anymore. She did because her mom loved his old movies. Scotty even wore the thick black-framed glasses, but he had a better build than the actor, and in Simone's opinion, was much better looking.

"Let me grab my racket." Amelia hurried toward her room. Seconds later, she yelled, "'Bye, Mom." Then she and Scotty were out the door.

Eric came up behind Simone and handed her the other dinner plates. "It's a nice night. Why don't we go for a swim and let the dishes soak? That way, we can work off some of the calories."

"Okay." She laughed. "I can stand to do a few laps in the pool."

She secured a plastic lid over the leftover lasagna and placed the covered dish in the fridge. While Eric finished clearing the table, she filled the sink with warm water and added dish soap.

"Be back in a few," Eric said, handing her the last dish.

Simone's gaze trailed him across the room as he left to grab his suit. It wasn't like Eric needed to watch his weight. He obviously outweighed Scotty, but his physique was more muscular; from the looks of it, he didn't seem to have an ounce of fat on him. What was it with men that they could eat just about anything and still look like that? It certainly wasn't fair.

Hurrying to her room to change, Simone couldn't wait to see him in a swimsuit. Of course, he'd get an eyeful when he saw her in a suit. He'd told her he liked women with curves. She definitely had a few of those.

Simone shucked her clothes and donned her modest one-piece suit. Still, as she glanced at her reflection in the mirror, one thought struck her. In over twelve years, she'd never purposely gone out with a guy while wearing practically nothing. Okay, not nothing compared to what most people wore nowadays.

She tugged at the straps. Observing her body, she waited for the fear to hit her, but it didn't. The only sensation swamping her was excitement. And that filled her with joy because her past was not hampering her present. She wanted her experience with Eric to be special, one not marred by bad memories.

Did that mean she wanted to make love with him? Goose bumps formed, but not totally due to the cool air blowing from the vent above. She rubbed her arms, quelling the fluttering in her stomach at her answer.

Yes.

In fact, the more she thought of it, the more the idea took up residence inside her brain and wouldn't budge. She grabbed her cover-up, threw it over her shoulders, and went to meet Eric.

On the way down the stairs, another thought emerged, this one more pressing. How did she go about letting Eric know she wanted him in that age-old way?

What a dilemma.

"Wow!" Eric's eyes filled with male admiration as she walked toward him.

Maybe she didn't need to do anything. He'd be the instigator?

She laughed and grabbed the hand he offered as they headed for the pool. "I brought towels."

It was still early and warm enough. They had the shaded pool to themselves since most of the sunbathers had gone inside. The others had gone from socializing in the pool area to socializing in a bar or restaurant. The condo complex held mostly singles and a few young couples with one small child. It definitely wasn't a place for large families.

"Race you to the diving board and back." Eric jumped into the inviting pool.

"You're on." Simone did a swimmer's dive. Once in the water, warmth surrounded her. She broke the surface and, noting Eric had a slight lead, increased her strokes.

In the end, her efforts did no good.

Laughing, Eric reached for her. "You're pretty fast. I had to work to win."

"I wouldn't want to make it easy for you."

By now they stood in the shallow end. A slight breeze blew, drawing goose bumps from her arms.

"You're cold." Eric reached out, but she splashed him.

"You're it." She dived underwater and kicked, propelling her to the left side of the pool where the water was deep enough that she had to stand on tiptoe to keep her head above water.

Eric had swooped beneath the surface and now tackled her, sending her sprawling and kicking in the water. She took a deep breath and held her nose, going under with a huge splash. When she broke the surface again, it was hard to keep from laughing.

The two continued playing tag. When Eric was *it*, he lunged for her. Simone laughed and dodged his grasp. She swam to the other side of the pool, keeping out of his reach until he eventually caught her.

"Finally, I have you right where I want you."

More laughter rose up when she splashed him again as he gripped her by the shoulders. She hadn't had this much fun in . . . well, in forever. It seemed she'd forgotten how to have fun. Really have fun. Eric was teaching her how all over again.

Simone could kiss him for that. The thought must have shown on her face because suddenly Eric's gaze zeroed in on her lips. She licked her top lip, then worried her bottom with her teeth. He groaned and pulled her closer.

"God, you're beautiful," he murmured right before lowering his mouth to hers.

Wet and hungry, they kissed. Only this time, Simone didn't stand on the sidelines and let it happen. She explored. Let her hands trail up his sinewy muscled arms and back down again. When that wasn't enough, she worked them up to his shoulder and finally wrapped them around his neck. Brought him closer. His desire lengthened between them, sending a thrill through her that was totally unexpected.

"Is that you, Mom?"

Amelia's voice registered. Like lead bars, Simone's arms dropped to her side. Still on tiptoe, she would have loved to have slipped under the water to avoid having to face her daughter. Unfortunately, Eric was firmly holding her at the waist.

With no choice, Simone glanced up at Amelia. Her daughter's pleased expression eased some of the embarrassment of being caught kissing like a couple of horny teens.

"Hi." She cleared her throat, then tossed a handful of wet hair behind her shoulders. "We were just . . . um . . . ."

"I know what you were doing, Mom." Amelia did one of her famous eye rolls that she had perfected over the last year. "Geez, I'm not a kid."

Scotty had the good sense to grab Amelia's hand and began pulling her away. "We'll meet you upstairs. We're ready for some cookies. Unlike some, who are having their dessert in the pool."

Once they were out of sight, Simone turned to Eric. "Well, now that I'm totally embarrassed, I guess I should get out."

"Not just yet." Eric's voice was teasing. "I'm not ready to let go of my dessert." His grip, still on her waist, tightened. "Wrap your legs around me and I'll carry you to the edge."

When she obeyed his command, he took two steps before he stopped. "First things first," he murmured into her ear. "I just need one more kiss." His mouth lowered over hers for what seemed like forever, when it was probably only a few seconds.

Simone didn't think she could ever tire of being on the receiving end of those lips. Eric Coleman knew how to kiss in a way that made her long for the next step.

He began walking again. With every step he took, his erection touched her in that private place that added to the yearning. At the pool's edge, he let go of her waist. In slow motion, she slid down his legs until her foot touched the bottom step.

Her cheeks flamed. She wasn't sure what to do to clue him in on how interested she was in what came next. It was like high school all over again, except at her age, she should be more knowledgeable.

Out of the corner of her eye, Simone spotted a black pickup in the parking lot and froze. God almighty, was she seeing threats where none existed?

Eric noticed her stiffen and his gaze narrowed. "What's wrong?"

"Nothing," she said quickly, not wanting to spoil the evening with would-be stalkers. She rubbed her arms. "I'm just cold. I didn't realize how chilly it's gotten."

Judging by his wary expression, her explanation didn't convince him. Going for a joviality that wouldn't seem forced, she reached for his hand and gave it a reassuring squeeze.

Then Simone leaned in to kiss him on the cheek. "Trust me. I enjoyed everything about tonight." She then stepped out of the pool and grabbed her towel. After drying off, she wrapped her hair in it turban-style and slipped into her cover-up.

Eric had wrapped the towel around his middle. All that did was highlight a very masculine chest, with muscles in all the right places to please any woman who appreciated those calendars with a different hunky man pictured each month.

Simone stared straight ahead as they walked side by side up to her condo. Every now and again, their bare legs would brush against each other. The entire trip up the stairs, she was aware of Eric.

Inside, Scotty and Amelia were at the table, a game board already laid out.

"It's about time you made it back." Amelia pointed to the board. "We were going to start without you."

Eric caught Simone's gaze, his eyes and curled lips full of teasing. "We'll finish the other later."

The memory of seeing the black pickup faded to the far reaches of her mind. Dreamily, she pulled out a chair and sat, not bothering to change out of her swimsuit. Doing so would take too much time, preventing her from savoring every moment Eric was in her house. The fact that Amelia was present added to her well-being.

When the game ended, Scotty and Amelia were the clear winners. Simone stood and rubbed her daughter's head. "Time for bed, sweetie."

"I should get going too." Scotty rose after picking up the game's pieces. He glanced at Amelia. "We're still on for tomorrow morning, right?"

"Yep. As long as your ego can handle it."

He chuckled. "Dream on, kid. I was going light on you. But no more Mr. Nice Guy. Tomorrow I'm going to kick ass."

Amelia tossed out a good-natured laugh. "Ooh. I'm quaking in my boots."

Simone was certain that nothing would happen to Amelia with Eric or Scotty around. In a few days, her daughter would be off at camp where she would be safe for the next three weeks. Then school would start shortly after she got home.

Everything would work out.

If Simone continued to see black pickups, she would gain Scotty's help in finding out who was tailing them. According to

Amelia, the guy was a whiz at such things.

Eric nodded to Scotty. "I promised to help with dishes."

Elated that Eric wasn't leaving just yet, Simone walked Scotty to the door. "Thanks for everything. You have no idea how much of an impact you've made on Amelia. She's a different kid this week." Mainly because her daughter was laughing and enjoying life, rather than being the sullen child who dreaded going to camp. "She's definitely more prepared for the next few weeks."

"I'll catch up with you at the office tomorrow," Eric told Scotty right before Simone closed the door.

"You don't have to stay." Wringing her hands as a sudden onset of nerves struck, Simone started for the kitchen. "It won't take long to finish."

"You don't want my company?" His teasing tone was back.

"I didn't say that." She turned around and saw that he'd followed her and was much too close. Her heart raced, and she was sure he could hear the thudding beats.

Both still wore bathing suits, but by now they were dry. Too much skin was showing for Simone to fully relax.

Eric trailed a finger up her arms. "I don't make you nervous, do I?"

"Yes. I mean, no." Simone pursed her lips, then said honestly, "Oh hell. I don't know." She pushed a strand of hair behind her ears and glanced at a spot on the floor to regain her equilibrium. For some reason, every time he got too close, her mind turned into one big blob and thinking was impossible. "This is all new to me."

She glimpsed his finger moving to her chin. He lifted it so she had to gaze into his eyes.

"Simone, I would never do anything to hurt you. Ever. Are we clear?"

Too choked up to speak, she cleared a grapefruit-sized lump from her throat and nodded. There was so much intensity in his eyes, and it was all she could do to keep herself from drowning in the warmth offered there. Of their own volition, her hands curled around his neck and brought his head lower. Feeling a little more confident, she traced his lips with her tongue.

He moaned and crushed her to him, and the kiss grew hot fast.

Eric was the first to break it. He hugged her to him and placed his chin on her head. "We need to slow down. Whenever I'm with you, I just want to be inside you. Which means I should leave. Wouldn't do for Amelia to find us in a more uncompromising position than she already has."

She giggled into his chest. It boggled her mind that he was actually taking the lead and worrying about her daughter rather than the other way around. When had that happened?

"Okay. Thanks, Eric. I had a wonderful evening with you."

Arm in arm, they walked to the door, and still Eric lingered, appearing in no hurry to leave. A thrill shot through her as she hoped he'd lingered to kiss her one last time.

She wasn't disappointed. Gentle hands drew her closer, and he bent until their lips met. This kiss was sweet and tender, and held the promise of things to come.

"Until tomorrow," he said. "Sleep tight."

And then Eric was striding away in the direction Scotty had gone just minutes before.

Simone closed her door. The loneliness that usually ate at her was totally gone, replaced with anticipation.

Another miracle.

As she headed for bed, she prayed for one more. That she could pull off sex with Eric without him guessing her shameful secret.

CHAPTER TWELVE

"THANKS FOR the update."

Senator Clifton Moorecroft disconnected the call that had interrupted a family dinner, and gazed at the photo on the laptop screen in front of him. The child was clearly his granddaughter; she had the Moorecroft chin and distinctive brow line. Though female, she resembled both his boys at the same age.

A sense of regret engulfed him. Too bad he couldn't claim Amelia as a Moorecroft. She was obviously a dynamo. As good at tennis as Blaine had been, and with Kent's smile, a kid like that would go far if given the right tools and education.

Such a pity. He had to forget about her and stay the course already in motion. As a father, it was his job to protect his sons. It wouldn't do him any good to dwell on the situation now. Blaine and Kent were the future and they both had children, so it wasn't as if Clifton didn't already have grandchildren. He'd do well to focus on the progeny he could acknowledge and not worry about the ones he couldn't. And he certainly wouldn't let something like this derail his plans.

When a knock sounded on his office door, he closed the laptop, stuck it in a side drawer, and locked it. "Come in."

Blaine stepped inside. "Everything okay?"

"Yes, of course. Come in for a moment."

Sitting up straight, Clifton set the key in the tray in front of him. Studying his son, he noted the redness in his eyes and the slight tremor in his hands. Blaine had been drinking more than usual lately, letting pressures get to him. Not good for a political candidate, and Clifton resolved to keep an eye on him. It wouldn't do for the heir apparent to fall apart and spoil all his father's plans.

"Have you polished your presentation for the donors' meeting tomorrow?"

His son nodded and gave him a wry smile. "If I spend any more time on it, I may wear a hole through it."

"One can never be too prepared." Clifton reached for the humidor on his desk and selected a cigar. He clipped the end, put it up to his mouth, and lifted his eyebrows in question at his son. "Do you mind? Your mother hates it when I light one up."

"She's just watching out for you." Blaine gave him an indulgent smile. "But go ahead. Having grown up smelling cigar smoke, it doesn't bother me—unlike your need to micromanage."

Clifton chuckled before he lit the cigar, then took an extended puff and shook out the match. Squinting at his son, he asked, "Is it a crime to want to ensure your success?"

"Isn't that Kent's job?"

"Bah!" Clifton blew the word out in an exhale of smoke. "He needs someone to go behind him to clean up his messes."

The door burst open and Kent stormed inside, clearly ready to go a few rounds, considering his red face and squared shoulders. "Having a meeting without me? What the hell, Dad?"

Clifton's only reaction was to calmly draw in a long puff on the cigar. On the exhale, he said, "I'm not sure I like the accusation in your voice, young man."

Sherlyn stepped up behind her husband and laid a warning hand on his shoulder. "Kent, please don't say anything rash."

Neither his father's rebuke nor his wife's request did anything to cool Kent's temper. He charged to his father's desk and slapped the top of it to make his point. "I'm Blaine's political adviser and need to be included in any meetings that pertain to getting him

91

elected."

Blaine shrugged. "It's not what you think. Basically Dad is just being Dad—you know? Making sure every *i* is dotted and every *t* is crossed."

"That's what I do." Clifton's patience eroded with each tamp of the cigar he'd lost the desire to smoke and was putting out in the ashtray. When it was completely out, he gave Kent a sharp look, unable to keep the anger out of his eyes. "Rest assured, I had no intention of stepping on your toes."

"I'll just bet," Kent said, glowering at his father.

"Kent, you're being unreasonable." Sherlyn gave her husband's arm a reassuring squeeze. "Your dad is only trying to help."

"I don't know why you're so angry." Blaine clearly struggled not to show his distaste, but the attempt did nothing to quell the caustic edge to his voice. "If anything, any help from Dad can only help your cause."

If a look could kill, the one Kent sent Blaine's way would have put him six feet under without digging a hole. "I never understood why Dad decided you'd make a better president."

Clifton sighed at their bickering. Blaine had never wanted to run for political office in the first place, and Kent was jealous. Always had been. He was impulsive and bitter, and never missed any opportunity to point out that Clifton had picked the wrong son to groom for a run at the White House.

"You know perfectly well why I chose Blaine." Clifton refrained from engaging in a verbal battle in front of his daughter-in-law, and kept his expression neutral as Kent sputtered.

"I can't help if I'm left in the dark."

"Rather than make a spectacle about something we can't change, let's work on making sure we're prepared for tomorrow." Clifton shot Kent a pointed look. "Does that meet with your approval?"

Another knock at the door drew his attention and he frowned.

Blaine's wife, Hope, poked her head inside. "We were wondering where you all disappeared to after dinner. This is supposed to be a family gathering. Mom told me to bring you all back to the dining room for dessert."

Clifton stood. "We're done here." With eyebrows raised, he glanced at Kent and then at Blaine. "We certainly don't want to disappoint your mother now, do we, boys?"

BLAINE LAGGED behind as Kent and his dad headed for the door to follow Hope out of the room.

His sister-in-law sidled up to him. "You should do more to make him understand you're not interested."

"It's easier said than done," he replied.

Sherlyn didn't have to say who and what she referred to. She knew Blaine hated politics and had never desired any of this. It was the main reason they'd broken up all those years ago in college—their dreams hadn't meshed.

He offered her a wry grin. "Do I detect a hint of regret for marrying the wrong brother?"

Sherlyn stiffened and the warmth fled from her expression. "Of course not. I love Kent. He'll go far, if given the chance."

Unaffected, Blaine nodded. He didn't have any hard feelings about their breakup or the fact that she'd latched onto Kent within weeks of it. His ambitious brother was exactly the type of man she needed. In return, Sherlyn had been a strong asset to Kent's campaign for the House seat he'd won. They were well matched.

What irony! Blaine might have laughed at one of his friends dealing with this dilemma. But it wasn't a friend's life, it was his, and it was anything but funny. If only their father could see that Kent was more suited for politics than him. Blaine hated the limelight. Kent loved it, and so did Sherlyn.

Unfortunately, his dad was like Kevlar. Impenetrable. Blaine had learned long ago to save his energy and resist fighting a losing battle.

"Dad knows more about what I want than I do," he said in an attempt to convince himself more than her. Hadn't his father introduced him to Hope? After two bad relationships with women he'd thought were above reproach, Blaine had discovered the hard way how flawed his judgment on finding a mate had been.

Hope was more sedate than Sherlyn and reminded Blaine of his mom. As Freudian as that was, he could see it in everything his wife did. She dressed to the nines and played the social game like a pro, but she was a quintessential homebody, always doing something to make their home Blaine's castle. It was what he loved most about her. He rather liked being considered king of his domain, the one place where his father's demands held no sway.

"Kent's made for the job." Sheryl's tone reflected her conviction. "At some point, that fact has to sink into that thick head of Clifton's."

"Apparently, my dad doesn't believe so. He's pretty stubborn, and isn't likely to change his mind without some strong persuasion."

"You just need to tell him forcefully that you're not his man." She wrapped her arm through his and slowly led him toward the door. "Besides, Dad likes me. I've been working on him, trying to get him to see the wisdom of Kent giving the White House a try instead of you. We've already bought a house in Virginia. When his congressional term is up, we'll wait a while and then he'll run for the Senate."

"In the meantime, maybe I'll lose my bid."

She shook her head. "You know that's unlikely."

"You're right. It will probably take a miracle to stop the wheels in motion." Blaine sighed and gave her a sideways glance. "I long for the good old days."

"Cheer up. You might just get your wish."

"What's keeping you?" Hope's teasing voice drew Blaine's attention. Her smile died when she spotted Sherlyn, who thankfully had the good sense to let go of his arm.

Smiling at him, Sherlyn whispered, "Tell him." Her throaty laugh rang in his ear as she walked away, saying over her shoulder to Hope, "Don't worry. I don't have any designs on your husband. I turned him down, remember?"

Yes, and she's a bitch for reminding Hope, Blaine thought, turning to his wife. Though a former beauty queen, she had insecurity issues, and he hated seeing her upset.

Hope's eyes practically snapped fire as she held his gaze. "What did she want?"

"She knows my heart isn't in the campaign, and encouraged me to talk to Dad."

She studied him for a moment, then squared her shoulders. "Good advice or not, it's too late to back out now."

"You're right, sweetheart." He bent to kiss the tip of her nose and her gaze softened. "We should catch up with the others. Mother is probably fit to be tied at the delay."

Although Hope wasn't the ambitious shark Sherlyn was, she definitely had her heart set on being a senator's wife. Which tightened the noose around his neck a little more each day.

Blaine walked a tightrope. Whether he won the election or lost it, he would disappoint someone he loved either way. And knowing that Simone Harris was back in town with a bomb that could destroy his political future was an added pressure that he sure as hell didn't need.

CHAPTER THIRTEEN

THURSDAY MORNING, Amelia was breathing heavily and about to hit a difficult shot when she spotted a black pickup truck parked across the parking lot. Ignoring the fact that she'd lost the point, she feigned tripping over her own feet and hobbled toward the net to get a better look.

A similar truck had been parked near her grandmother's house yesterday. Was it following her? Despite the warm morning breeze, a chill rose up her spine at the thought.

Scotty rushed toward her. "Are you okay?"

"Yes." She grabbed his arm, acting as if she needed support, and lowered her voice. "Don't look up. Look at my knee and pretend like you're concerned, and then check out that truck behind me. But don't let on what you're doing."

Scotty did as she asked. "Okay. Now what?"

"I think that black truck's been following me."

His expression immediately turned from curious to grave. He swiped at the back of his neck and took another look at the truck. This time his focus lingered as his gaze narrowed. "Are you sure?"

Amelia shook her head. "Not totally, but I don't want to make a mistake of not paying attention to my mom's sixth sense. She's been nervous lately."

Scotty glanced back at the ground. "Okay, here's what we'll do.

You've already faked an injury, so we'll pretend we're done for the day." Scotty reached around her shoulders. "Grab on, hop on one foot, and make it look good."

Exhaling a relieved sigh, Amelia nodded. "Good idea."

Hopping on one foot, she allowed him to guide her to the staircase in Eric's building, which was closer than hers. Now around the corner and out of sight of the truck, Scotty released her. They scrambled up the stairs and hurried toward Eric's unit only to find a woman outside his door, about to knock.

Considering those familiar dark good looks, she had to be related to Eric, with shiny coal-black hair that swung past her shoulders, and matching expressive dark eyebrows that winged over big brown eyes the color of chocolate. It was bad enough that a guy had those gorgeous eyes with amazing eyelashes, but on a woman? Crap, that just made Amelia feel dowdy and plain.

"Can we help you?" Scotty reached into his pocket and pulled out a set of keys.

"I was looking for Eric." The woman pursed her lips as she studied them. "You know, hoping he might be home." She held out a hand. "I'm Trish. Eric's sister."

"I'm Scotty." Grinning, he nodded as he took her hand and held it. "He went into work early today."

"Darn." She offered him a wan smile. "I meant to catch him before he left."

"Scotty," Amelia said, interrupting what looked to be two adults making goo-goo eyes at each other. She might be young, but she recognized mutual attraction when she saw it. *Why did adults have to act so boring towards each other?*

Sending her elbow into his arm, Amelia said pointedly, "Remember the truck?"

"Oh yeah." His grin turned sheepish and he dropped Trish's hand. "I almost forgot. Why don't you come inside? Maybe you can help us."

Pink hit Trish's cheeks as she tucked a strand of hair behind her ear. "I'm not sure how, but I'm willing to try."

Scotty dragged his gaze away to concentrate on opening Eric's front door. Once inside, he acted as if he hadn't been eyeing Trish as if she were a plate of hot, salty, steaming French fries and he'd been on one of those stupid diets for weeks. "We need to figure out a way to get the truck's license plate number without the driver suspecting he's been made."

"It could be nothing," Amelia warned, praying that it was. She spent a moment explaining in greater detail what had happened on that scary day as both listened intently. "A truck like the one parked outside almost forced us off the road. Afterward, we saw a black pickup in Norcross everywhere we turned." She swallowed the knot of fear that had lodged in her throat and added, "But black pickups are everywhere, and I'm probably being paranoid just like my mom."

Scotty frowned. "Keeping your eyes open to threats isn't paranoia. It's smart. Especially these days."

"He's right," Trish said with a nod. "There are a lot of crazies out there. I should know. I've met my fair share."

"There's one way to find out." Amelia took out her cell phone. "I'm calling my grandmother. When she comes to pick me up, if the pickup follows me, then we'll know for sure."

Grinning, Scotty rubbed his hands together. "I'm up for it," he said at the same time Trish said, "Maybe I can help. Like get a tag number, since no one knows me."

He and Trish exchanged phone numbers and agreed to meet at a coffee shop around the corner once Amelia's grandmother picked her up.

Silence settled around them until Trish said, "I wanted to be a tennis pro." Her nod indicated their rackets. "And then I grew up and faced reality. Kids like me didn't go to those famous tennis camps. They got messed up instead."

Amelia scrunched up her nose. "You don't look messed up."

Trish laughed. "Let's just say I'm a work in progress." She turned to leave. "I'll go on ahead and get into position to see if the pickup follows you. That'll give me a chance to get a license number without the guy knowing we're on to him."

"Great." Scotty opened the door for her. "By the way, I'm always open to new partners. Anytime you want to play, just text me or give me a call."

"I will," she murmured, hurrying past him.

When Trish left, Amelia fidgeted, fighting to remain relaxed.

Scotty offered her a comforting smile. "Don't worry. You and your mom can count on us. Nothing will happen to you on my watch."

His promise took the weight of the world off her shoulders. Amelia reached out and hugged him. "Thanks, Scotty."

Somehow she felt safer now, which made her realize just how afraid she'd been these last several weeks.

<><><>

SCOTTY SIPPED his coffee, acting as if waiting for a hot babe to join him was an everyday occurrence. Yet every nerve ending in his body was on high alert as Trish made her way to his table with her latte. Why had Eric never mentioned a sister?

The brunette knockout, a female version of Eric with the same dark eyes and coal-black hair, drew second glances from every guy in the place. Scotty was the first to admit he stood at the head of the line of gawkers. Yet the woman intrigued him for more than just her looks.

Sadness lurked in her eyes. Trish probably had no idea she projected it. Hell, he had no idea how he'd been able to discern it from the couple of glimpses in those few moments they'd spent talking. Seeing her now, he began to doubt his earlier assessment.

"The pickup might well have been following Amelia. But I'm not positive." Trish pulled out a chair directly across from him and sat. "When Grandma drove off, the black truck waited several minutes before making a U-turn and heading in the opposite direction."

"Hmm." Scotty refocused on the reason they were meeting and stared at a spot beyond Trish's shoulder, thinking. "Maybe she's not paranoid at all. It seems too much of a coincidence."

Sin had a saying about coincidences. There were none. Scotty tended to agree with that philosophy.

"I was able to get the license number." Trish's pleased voice yanked his attention back to that beautiful face. "It was a Georgia plate."

The excited gleam in her eye was contagious. Scotty met her smile with one of his own.

"It shouldn't take too long to figure out who this stalker is."

He plugged the number into his cell phone. Once at the office, he could log on to the secure URL he'd created for extracting similar information for the government. It wouldn't hurt to use the site for his own purposes. After all, the guy could be a kidnapper, and with a Georgia plate, might plan to transport his victim across state lines. That would put the case squarely under the purview of the FBI, which was good enough rationalization for him.

Done typing, Scotty glanced back at Trish, who now eyed him curiously. Her flicker of interest caught him off guard with its intensity, and sent a surge of warmth straight to his groin. He sat up taller and worked to contain the excitement running through his system that took every ounce of control he had. *Wouldn't do to seem overeager.*

Women like Trish seldom gave geeky guys like him the time of day; unless, of course, they needed something. Experience had taught him that. His ex had only wanted to marry him to attain citizenship. Once she had it, she filed for divorce. When the divorce was final, she and their baby had disappeared and were living under the radar. No amount of digging had unearthed her location.

Yet, in this instance, Trish might just be the exception. Scotty definitely planned to use that to his advantage and get to know her.

"Would you like to have lunch sometime?" The question burst out before he could second-guess the wisdom of it, despite his attempts to remain aloof and cool.

Her brows knitted together. "Sure." Trish paused. "When?"

"How about today," he said, giving up all pretense of trying to act disinterested.

She shook her head. "I can't. How about tomorrow," she offered, which was much better than being rejected outright. "Where should I meet you?"

"I'll pick you up." He smiled, going for broke. "Around noonish. Where do you work?"

Trish pursed her lips and glanced down at her hand on her

coffee cup. Seconds passed before she cleared her throat. "I'm between jobs right now." She shrugged. "So noonish is fine."

Scotty cocked his head to one side, studying her. "Does that mean you're looking for work?"

"Yeah."

"What type of work are you interested in?"

"I'm a personal assistant. Or at least that was my last title before I was let go."

"Hmm." The wheels in his head spun as he tried to figure out a way to capitalize on this opportunity.

"Don't tell Eric, okay?" She frowned and those gorgeous eyes of hers pleaded. "Our relationship is still pretty shaky. I'd prefer to wait until I have another job lined up before admitting to being unemployed."

"Okay." He had no idea why she didn't want Eric to know, but that was between brother and sister. "I know someone looking for an admin assistant. Light typing. Filing and good phone skills. I'll give him your name and tell him to expect your call." He took out a pen and small notebook he always carried and jotted down the information. "Don't wait too long to call, though."

Trish took the piece of paper and stared at it for a few seconds before returning her gaze to him. "You'd do that for me?"

"Of course." When she looked at him like that, he could see himself promising her more than just a lead to a job interview. "But you'll have to sell yourself. And I'll warn you, he's a little picky."

"Thanks. You're a lifesaver." Her smile was more than genuine. It held warmth.

Scotty's posture stretched even higher, making him feel six inches taller than his five-foot-eight-inch frame. "In the meantime, how about helping me watch out after Amelia and her mom for a couple of days?"

As with the suggestion of a lunch date, the question just popped out. Geez, he hoped she didn't think him overzealous. Still, the more he thought about it, the better he liked the idea. Hopefully, she would too. His offer would serve two purposes— help her out, which might aid in his desire to get to know her, and help out his new tennis partner. Win-win.

"I'd pay you the same as I would a private investigator," he added.

"It's a deal." Another smile lit her face. "I'll start on it right away."

"Great." He looked at his watch. *Damn.* He was going to be late for his ten o'clock meeting if he didn't get a move on. "I hate to cut this short, but I gotta run."

Besides staking out the grandmother's house, Trish agreed to be on hand in the morning when he and Amelia played tennis to see if the truck showed up again. If so, she'd stick on its tail to see if it was following Amelia. They agreed to compare notes on her detective work the next day at lunch.

Traffic was still heavy as Scotty sped toward the office. He zipped around a semi and veered off I-295, barely avoiding a merging car in an effort to make it in on time.

As he stepped off the elevator, he almost bumped into Eric.

"Hey, you're just the person I was hoping to run into."

Eric's eyebrows shot up. "Oh?"

"Yeah, and I have you to thank, since you're related."

Eric pulled a face. "Tell me you're not talking about my sister, Trish?"

"The one and only. She stopped by, looking for you." Scotty relayed what had happened with the pickup and Trish's part in it. "After Amelia left, we got together for coffee. It's why I'm so late."

"For hell's sake, Scotty. I'm still not sure about Trish. She could very well be trouble with a capital T. At least steer clear of her until I feel better about her."

"But she offered her help. And she's your sister."

"Half sister."

"Still, she's family. Doesn't that mean anything?"

"In my family, it means she could turn on you in a heartbeat." A harsh expression stole over Eric's face. "And I don't want to see you hurt."

"I'm a big boy and can take care of myself." Scotty ground his teeth in an effort to remain calm. "But thanks for the heads-up."

Eric grunted. "Don't say I didn't warn you." He jabbed the elevator button with more force than necessary. "By the way, Sin's having us all over for a barbecue tomorrow night to help me out with Simone and Amelia. You're invited too, so put it on your calendar and don't be late."

"Can I invite Trish?"

"Why?"

"To get to know her better. Isn't that what you're suggesting I do?"

"Don't say I didn't warn you if she breaks your heart. Trish is a female me. After all, we learned from the best."

"She's helping me keep the kid safe, and she deserves to be there." Scotty held his head high, his mulish expression daring Eric to question his motives.

"Suit yourself." Eric's lips curled into a snarl. "I can lead a horse to water, but if he turns into a jackass who won't drink, it's time to bow out." He turned to step inside the elevator.

"This jackass will do what he damn well pleases, thank you very much."

The doors closed and Scotty stormed toward his office, wondering why Eric had a burr up his butt about Trish. What Scotty wouldn't give to see his own sister—but the chances of that happening were about as remote as a person finding water in the Mojave Desert in July.

At his desk, Scotty slumped into his chair and picked up his messages. Great. His ten o'clock meeting had been pushed back an hour. He swiveled to glance out his floor-to-ceiling windows with a bird's-eye view of the parking lot. As he studied the few people exiting their cars and heading toward the building, his thoughts turned to Amelia's stalker.

Hell, he wasn't even sure it was a stalker. It could be coincidence. Now that he had a few minutes, it would be a good time to find out about the license plate.

After spending several minutes online, he was no further ahead with learning the identity of the mystery pickup than when he'd started. The truck was a rental, leased to an "M. Cullen." Researching further, he found an address and then a phone number, which he promptly called. An automated voice answered on the second ring.

Without leaving a message, Scotty hung up.

The call hadn't yielded what he'd hoped for. Googling the address was even more disappointing and led him to a vacant lot. The name could easily be an alias, leading him back to the beginning. Until he and Trish had more information, he'd hold off on alerting Simone. Amelia was either with her mother, grandmother, or him, so there wasn't much a stranger could do. Especially now that Amelia was on the alert.

Des and Eric tended to act first and ask questions later. That might cause a bit of embarrassment to all involved if it was indeed a coincidence. Then Sin would be pissed at Scotty for instigating it with false leads.

Hopefully he'd have a solid lead by the time they all got together for the barbecue tomorrow night. Or at least enough information that Scotty would feel comfortable letting the matter drop.

<><><>

SIMONE MET Michael for lunch at La Boulangerie. The restaurant had become their hangout over the last few days. The food was enjoyable. Unfortunately, the company wasn't. The more time she spent with Michael, the more she compared him to Eric and found him lacking. The last forty-five minutes spent talking with him had only reinforced her opinion.

Simone headed back to work intending to end things. It wasn't fair to lead Michael on. Of course, she wasn't sure that's what she was doing; after all, they were only friends. Yet deep down inside, she sensed he was looking for more than she could give.

As she rushed through the rest of her day, the idea of spending more time with Michael, for lunch or otherwise, didn't sit well with her. She needed to do something about it.

Once the workday ended, Simone stopped at her mother's house to pick up Amelia. She found the two in their usual spot, out on the deck. Lorraine was reading and Amelia was playing with Buttons.

Lorraine set down her book and looked up. "How was your

date last night?"

"Fine." Her use of the word date hadn't gone unnoticed. Instead of correcting her mom, Simone couldn't contain the grin that broke out just at the memory of the night. "In fact, we're getting together tonight."

Amelia had been walking on air, so excited about all Scotty was teaching her. Simone couldn't help but offer another night of dinner for another night of lessons. Scotty had readily agreed, but had insisted on providing the food. He'd opted for pizza. Eric had seconded the plans.

"You're welcome to come," Simone offered, knowing both men would be very accommodating. Another feather for Eric's cap, she thought.

"Oh, no." Lorraine stood. "I have my book club meeting tonight." As she headed for the house, she said over her shoulder, "I'm pleased that you're actually seeing someone."

"So am I." Simone hugged her middle. Six months ago, it would have been unfathomable to picture herself in a relationship, to imagine being excited over a man.

Simone followed her mother inside. "By the way, Mom," she said, helping her prepare drinks. "We're all invited to a barbecue tomorrow night. Eric's partner has a son Amelia's age. Eric included you in the invite. I know it's short notice, but I thought you might like to meet them. This would be a perfect opportunity."

"That's sweet of you to think of me, but I don't want to impose."

"Don't be silly. It's supposed to be a party. The more, the merrier. You're coming. If I can go, you can go. We'll just take extra food."

Lorraine's smile grew. "Sounds wonderful. I would like to meet these paragons who've captivated both my girls."

Simone nodded as another thought formed. Eric and his friends *had* wormed their way into not only her life, but also her daughter's, and were well on the way to including her mother.

The idea warmed her heart and had to mean something. Ordinarily, Simone would never have allowed such a crossover. That alone was proof enough that their relationship was meant to be.

She couldn't wait until she saw Eric again.

CHAPTER FOURTEEN

S IMONE COULDN'T quell the excitement bursting from her smile when she opened the door to Eric carrying a huge bowl of salad. Behind him, Scotty held two pizza boxes. As she stepped aside to let them pass, garlic and tomato sauce assaulted her nostrils.

"Smells heavenly." Her stomach gurgled. "I'm starving."

"So am I." Amelia relieved Scotty of his burden. At the table she set them down, then opened the top box and sniffed. Her gaze lifted toward the heavens. "The works. My kind of pizza."

Scotty nodded. "And for the picky eater, I ordered one with half pepperoni and half plain cheese."

"You thought of everything." Simone grinned, not a fan of the peppers and onions Amelia loved.

As before, they sat around the table Simone had set earlier. The pizza disappeared fast as four hungry eaters consumed it with gusto.

Amelia took one last bite, set the piece of crust down, and scooted her chair back. "I'm done for now," she said after swallowing. Then grinning, she added, "I'll have another piece after I beat Scotty."

Scotty threw down his napkin and shoved away from the table. "Dream on, kid. No more Mr. Nice Guy. I'm bringing out the big guns."

Their banter continued as they exited the front door, leaving a comfortable silence in their wake.

"So . . ." Eric picked up his wineglass and took a sip. Setting the glass down, he said, "Alone again. At last."

Simone nodded, suddenly too tongue-tied to speak. Why was she nervous around him when all day, she'd looked forward to the thought of being alone with him? Would she ever be normal? Obviously, Blaine's actions were still affecting her, even though she'd done much to overcome them.

"Are you okay, Simone?"

Eric's question pulled her out of her thoughts and she offered a wobbly smile, wondering if being whole again were even possible. "I'm fine."

He rose to his feet to take her hand and tug her out of her chair. As she stood, he pushed a strand of hair behind her ear. His touch was featherlight as the back of his hand brushed up and down the side of her face. With thumb and forefinger on her chin, he lifted her head so she had to gaze into his eyes that were filled with an intensity she'd come to expect.

"Remember my promise?" His eyebrows rose. "I'll never do anything to hurt you."

Her confidence returned as the memory of last night entered her thoughts. Feeling bolder, she offered her best siren's smile, wrapped an arm around his neck to bring him closer, and traced his lips with her tongue. A déjà vu moment, to be sure.

Eric didn't disappoint. Just as last night, he groaned and crushed her to him. Their mouths melded together.

Like a fire that had been smoldering too long, flames of desire erupted within Simone's belly. She loved the wild and erotic sensations filling her.

Same as before, Eric broke the kiss, much to her disappointment. If it had been up to her, she would have made love with him on the spot. *Maybe I'm more normal than I thought.* The idea made her smile into his broad chest as he hugged her to him and placed his chin on her head.

"Damn," he whispered. "I'm dying to be inside you. It's getting harder and harder to resist you when you kiss me like that." He leaned back and glanced down at her, honesty blazing from his eyes. "But I want us to be more than a one-night stand." He cleared his throat. "Let's finish the dishes. We can wait until Amelia is off at tennis camp to finish this."

"You're right."

Simone suppressed a laugh. Imagine, she actually had a life outside of being a mom. Usually the thought of Amelia leaving left her depressed, but tonight she found she was looking forward to having two weeks without her daughter. That in itself was a miracle.

She gave Eric a fierce hug, let go, and headed for the kitchen as he followed. After they made quick work of the dishes, Simone pointed to the bottle on the counter.

"There's still a little wine, if you'd like another glass."

"I'd love nothing better." The heated look he sent her made her think he wasn't talking about drinking wine.

She poured, handed him his glass, then picked up her own.

"Here's to fate bringing us together."

Laughing, Simone clinked glasses with him. "I rather like the thought of fate bringing us together."

Wine in hand, they made their way to sofa and sat. After a few minutes of small talk, he set his wineglass down on the coffee table, relieved her of her wine and set it next to his, then placed his hands on her shoulders. A thrill shot through her when she realized his full intent.

There was a teasing glint in his eyes. "I can't resist sneaking one more kiss."

Her insides heated and her gaze moved from his eyes to those full lips. "I'd like that," she whispered.

In slow motion she leaned into him, totally aware that Eric was the only man she'd ever been this intimate with other than . . . *No. That bastard has stolen too much, and he isn't stealing this moment.*

Besides, Eric wasn't just any man. He was someone she'd come to trust.

Of its own volition, her mouth opened in invitation. He didn't hesitate to take her up on it and wrap his arms around her.

The instant their lips touched, it was as if she'd died and gone to heaven for the second time that evening. Warmth she'd never felt before engulfed her, and she never wanted the feeling to end. Eventually it did when he raised his head.

"God, you're beautiful." Those soulful eyes searched hers. "You know that?"

She reached out to touch the side of his face and ran the back of her hand up and down before stroking his hair. "So are you."

"Maybe we've each met our match?" He pressed his forehead to hers, still breathing heavily.

"Maybe." Heavens, wouldn't that be—

"Mom, Scotty's going to show me a few moves on my game."

Too engrossed in Eric, Simone hadn't realized Amelia and Scotty had just burst through the front door after playing tennis. Flustered, she jerked to a full sitting position and ran a hand through her hair to compose herself. At the same time, Eric grabbed a sofa pillow and plopped it over his obvious erection.

"Eric had something caught in his eye," she said quickly, unable to meet Amelia's eye.

The lie came out so easily that Simone wondered if that made her a bad person. There had to be some rule somewhere that said *no lying to your kids*. Even white lies that protected them from emotional stuff they weren't ready for were probably forbidden. Still, she added one more.

"I was trying to see what it was."

Thank God Amelia was laughing at something Scotty said and didn't seem to notice her embarrassment or her comment.

"We won't be too long," her daughter added as they both headed toward the computer room.

"Okay." Simone sent up a prayer of gratitude on two counts. One that Amelia was oblivious to having interrupted a heated moment, and another that she had a few more minutes to spend with Eric.

It wasn't lost on her that having never experienced this type of situation before—namely her daughter's interruption during heated moments—she had to be more careful, especially since it kept happening. That alone was something to think about as well as relish.

For the life of her, she didn't know what was worse. Knowing there was more and having to wait, or having no clue as to what she was waiting for.

Oh, for heaven's sake. How could she even compare the two? Being a clueless loner was the most unappealing thing a person could be. How had she ever lived so long as one?

Well, no more.

In that moment, Simone decided she'd make very good use of her daughter's absence while Amelia was away at camp. Eric Coleman wouldn't know what hit him.

Smiling to herself, she gave him a studied glance, wondering how to best go about seducing him during Amelia's absence.

Of course, judging by what happened earlier, he probably thought he was seducing her.

CHAPTER FIFTEEN

S IMONE WOKE well before her alarm rang. Energized and too excited to go back to sleep, she sprang out of bed.

Time seemed to drag before she and Amelia finally walked to the tennis courts where they found Scotty hitting balls against the backboard.

Bending to kiss Amelia good-bye, Simone said, "Don't forget, we're going to dinner tonight with Eric and Scotty's friends."

"Sure, Mom. Have a good day."

On the walk to the Metro station, Simone glanced around. After a solid fifteen seconds of intense surveillance without spying anything that remotely looked like a black pickup, she heaved a relieved sigh and practically skipped the rest of the way.

The twenty-minute trip went by in a blur as memories of last night's kisses filled her with warmth. She was beginning to fall in love with Eric. He was such a romantic. He wanted her. That much had been certain, considering his telltale erection.

She'd wanted him too. Unfortunately, for her it wasn't as easy as just hopping into bed. She had Amelia to think about. Not only that, her last sexual encounter had been a nightmare. Despite having little memory of the night other than in foggy bits and pieces, it had been her one and only dip into the sex arena.

Her biggest worry wasn't sleeping with Eric, but rather hiding the fact of her lack of experience. Oh, why hadn't she dated more? Still, nothing would sway her from her goal of having Eric for a lover. Of course she wanted more, namely a lasting relationship, but making love would be a wonderful beginning.

She walked up the ascending escalator leading out the Metro, suddenly in a hurry to get on with her day. A block later, she was at her office building.

Once inside and seated at her desk, she remembered her lunch date with Michael and cringed. The thought of making small talk with him after last night with Eric was as appealing as a trip to the dentist.

There was only one thing to do. She reached for the phone.

He answered on the second ring. "Hi, beautiful."

"Hi, Michael." She cleared her throat and blurted, "I can't get away for lunch today." She crossed her fingers, hating herself for telling little white lies. "I've got too much work to do."

Simone exhaled the breath she'd been holding when he said, "I understand deadlines."

They made a date for the following Monday. Simone hung up, wishing she'd had the nerve to just end things completely.

While placing her purse in the bottom drawer, she realized they had nothing in common, so even being friends with the man held little appeal.

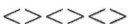

HE DISCONNECTED the call, quelling an overwhelming urge to throw the cell phone out the window. He hit the steering wheel instead. Twenty minutes later, after watching the brat play tennis, his irritation hadn't eased. In fact, emotions were getting the better of him. Again.

His patience for completing the job was nonexistent. That he had an impatient client only compounded the problem. If he didn't wrap up this gig soon, he would end up doing something stupid.

Same as always, the grandmother drove into the lot to pick up the kid. He checked the time. Punctual enough to set his watch to her arrival, he thought, putting his truck into gear and following at a safe distance.

For weeks now, he'd surveyed his targets' comings and goings. Simone was a loner with a definite routine who rarely went out. Tonight, the information he'd gleaned would pay off.

Was that a tail? The notion chilled him to the bone. After noting the same car several times in the rearview mirror, he couldn't be sure. Now a block from Grandma's house, he turned off, then slowed to a stop at the curb. When the car passed by without turning, he wiped his sweaty palms on his pants.

He might be safe now, but exposure could happen at any time. That meant only one thing. Taking care of business tonight was paramount.

He drove toward his hotel, not bothering with any more surveillance.

Simone had begged off lunch with her new friend for today, and had rescheduled for Monday. Too bad she wouldn't be around to keep her date. Michael caught his reflection in the rearview mirror and grinned, visualizing the moment just before her death when he would reveal himself.

No one would guess that her killer was someone she knew.

SCOTTY MET Trish for lunch at a Mexican hole-in-the-wall not too far from his office. The place was a dive, but they served one hell of a burrito, and Trish had mentioned she loved Mexican food.

When their order came up, they found an empty table outside. He helped her into her seat before grabbing the chair across from her and sitting.

After taking a few bites, Trish put down her burrito and wiped at her mouth. "This is really good."

Scotty nodded. They ate in silence until curiosity got the better of him. "What do you have?" he asked, getting to the reason for meeting.

"Not much. This morning the black pickup was there, just like

114

yesterday. This time I followed him. He turned off on a street a block from Amelia's grandmother's house. I even staked out that house until just before I drove here, and nada. I'm not totally sure the truck's presence was coincidence or if he was following them."

"My money's on the latter. Good job." He took out his wallet. "How many hours did you work?"

Trish put her hand over his and shook her head. "Rather than money, I was hoping for a favor."

The touch of her hand was electrifying. Scotty's heart stopped. For a moment he forgot how to breathe.

"Are you okay?" Trish's gaze narrowed as she studied him.

He laughed off the feeling. "Sure." Now that his lungs worked, he took a deep breath. "What did you have in mind?"

How would it be if she said she wanted him?

Dream on, Scotty, the negative voice in his mind said with a sneer. It sounded an awful lot like his ex-wife. *You wouldn't know what to do with her if she did that.*

Yes, I would, his subconscious shouted back. *I'd take much better care of her than the guy she's seeing now.*

Trish had let it slip that she had a boyfriend, a real downer of a revelation. But it didn't matter. Scotty was determined to be her friend because she needed one. Not just a man who took what her body offered, but one who actually appreciated the other aspects of her personality, like her mind and . . . okay . . . she did have a mighty fine ass.

Just help her out and don't expect anything, he told himself. For crying out loud, he wasn't some Neanderthal with more brawn than brains.

Don't forget what happened the last time you helped out a hot babe.

He'd ended up with a broken heart. That fact he couldn't argue away.

I'll be careful.

"Scotty? Are you sure you're okay? You look a little funny."

"I'm fine." He went for a confident smile that was hard to pull off, considering he'd been arguing with himself rather than paying attention to the problem at hand. "You were about to ask for a favor?"

"Well—" She broke off and tore at a paper napkin on the table in front of her.

Just as she'd done a moment ago, Scotty placed his hand over hers. Again, he felt a spark of attraction that zinged straight to his heart, but he ignored it. "Go on. I'm listening."

"You know Eric and I share the same dad, right?"

When Scotty nodded, she shrugged. "He isn't doing so hot right now. He's already had one major stroke and is resisting treatment. No telling how long he has, not with all the strikes against him. I mean, he still smokes a pack a day, or he would if they'd let him. He's missing an eye due to cancer. His body has been ravaged from alcohol and drug abuse." She stopped to take a breath, then offered him a woeful smile. "He's asked to see Eric, but Eric doesn't want anything to do with him."

"What does that have to do with me?"

Even though he asked, Scotty already had a sneaking suspicion of what that was. It wasn't his place to interfere in Eric's life. Scotty had gotten to know Eric pretty well during the past year while helping him improve his reading skills.

His friend wasn't anything like the shallow guy Scotty had pegged him to be after first meeting him. Eric was loyal to a fault and gave of himself in a way that wasn't obvious. He was also kind and had a soft spot for animals.

"You're his friend. I was hoping you could talk him into it."

Scotty frowned and was about to refuse when she said, "Please. There's unfinished business between them."

"Eric knows his own mind. I doubt I can change it."

"You need to try. For his sake. I've had enough therapy to recognize a few things. My brother will never be happy with himself until he comes to terms with his past, and that means seeing his dad for who and what he was. And more importantly, forgiving him. Not for my dad's sake, but for his own peace of mind. Otherwise, Eric will continue to have a hard time with intimacy."

"I see." Scotty mulled her comments a bit. Eric didn't believe in all the psycho-babble shit—Eric's words, not his, that Trish was espousing. Except she made sense.

"All I can do is talk to him."

Then remembering Eric's comment about leading a jackass to water, Scotty smiled. Maybe he should do a little more than talk. He should be the one to lead the jackass to the source.

"Don't worry, Trish. I appreciate your concern and I'll do what I can. He's my friend, and I want to see him happy and unencumbered by the past too."

Her smile brightened his day.

SIMONE RUSHED out of the Metro stop, happy to be free for the weekend. She'd taken off a few hours early in order to prepare potato salad for tonight. Her mom would pick Simone up around six thirty for the drive to Sin and Avery's house. Eric had texted directions earlier and would meet them there.

The two-block walk to her condo complex didn't take long. At the corner, her gaze swept the street. When nothing caught her attention, she continued her scrutiny throughout the parking lot.

Outside her unit, she quickly unlocked the door and sent up a silent thank-you to the heavens that there were no black pickups in sight.

After a quick change into skinny jeans and a blue silk blouse that Amelia said "looked awesome on her," Simone grabbed an apron and went to work in the kitchen. Her mom was bringing pasta salad and a fruit salad. Between the two of them, they had the salads covered.

At first, Simone stayed too busy organizing ingredients and setting pans of eggs and potatoes to boil on the stove to think about the evening ahead.

Once done, however, daydreams about Eric and his kisses played out in her mind's eye. She smiled. Giddy excitement filled her, and she practically danced around the condo in anticipation.

She completed the mundane task of peeling the boiled potatoes and cutting them into squares, then glanced at her watch. Darn. It was only five thirty. Time seemed to be passing at a snail's pace.

Simone wiped her hands on her apron, reached for one of the cooled hard-boiled eggs, and cracked the shell.

When done with chopping, she blended the eggs, onions, and mayo, added a squirt of mustard along with seasoned salt, and finished blending. She covered the bowl with plastic wrap and set it in the fridge to cool.

At 6:25, Amelia texted that they were waiting in the parking lot.

Sweater on her arm and the salad in hand, Simone hurried out the door, stopping only the few seconds it took to lock it.

<><><>

MICHAEL STOOD in the early evening shadows, waiting. And watching. As soon as Simone was out of sight, he nonchalantly strode toward her door. Seconds later, he was inside. A quick search of the condo yielded a balcony that had two sliding glass door accesses—one from the master bedroom and one from the living room.

He moved to the door in the bedroom, which had been left closed yet unlatched, and stepped outside. It was a long drop to the ground level, but there were plenty of other ways down for a fast exit. Just in case. He always had a contingency plan. As he'd already discovered, this case required one.

Now all Michael had to do was wait. Using every bit of the patience he possessed, he made himself comfortable to do just that.

<><><>

THE DRIVE to Sin and Avery's neighborhood took about twenty-five minutes, giving Simone a bit of time to think.

"Wow. Get a load of these houses, Mom."

The mini-mansions were intimidating, reminding Simone of Blaine's home. Or rather, his parents' home. Eric's condo had to be similar to her humble unit and made her originally think he didn't have that kind of money. But if he was an equal partner in his business, he most likely did.

Maybe he could help her if the black pickup had something to do with the Moorecrofts realizing they had a granddaughter living in their midst. She didn't see how that scenario would play out when the father on Amelia's birth certificate was listed as "unknown." Besides, she highly doubted they gave a hoot. Not after the way they told her to end her pregnancy. Yet, Simone hadn't hidden Amelia's birth either, so it was possible.

Her thoughts were interrupted when her mother turned into the circular driveway and came to a stop.

"We're here." Lorraine offered her a quick smile. "You have some interesting friends, sweetie."

"Friends of friends," she said, climbing out and reaching for the potato salad.

"Here, Amelia," her mother said once out of the car. "Take the fruit salad and I'll take the pasta salad."

The trio walked up the grand staircase that led to a grand porch. As soon as they reached the grand door, it opened. Grand seemed to be the only word that worked.

"You made it." Eric relieved Simone of the potato salad and leaned in for a quick kiss on the cheek. He turned to her mother and grinned. "Mrs. Morgan, I presume? It's nice to meet you. I'm Eric Coleman. Simone has told me all about you."

"Call me Lorraine."

Eric shook the hand she offered, took her bowl too, and nodded toward a hallway. "Let me put these in the kitchen. Then I'll introduce you to the gang. Amelia, come with me and I'll show you where that goes."

As Amelia trailed behind Eric, Simone and her mom gravitated toward voices.

A woman came into view with an outstretched hand. "You must be Simone."

Shaking hands, Simone offered her a genuine smile. "And you must be Avery."

Avery was dressed in skinny jeans and a silk blouse—an everyday outfit much like Simone's—except this woman looked as if she'd just stepped off the runway in Paris. Avery Sinclair fit the house. Beautiful, but not overdone or pretentious. Simone liked her right away.

Avery turned to Lorraine. "I gather you're Simone's mom, Mrs. Morgan? Although you look more like her sister."

"Hmph." Lorraine grinned. "I feel more like her grandmother

these days, but thank you for such a nice compliment."

"This is Andy, my son," Avery said, indicating a boy about Amelia's age, who'd come to stand behind her during the introductions.

By now Amelia had deposited her burden in the kitchen and was entering the room along with two men, most likely Eric's partners.

Avery smiled. "This is my husband, Jeff, but everyone calls him Sin."

Sin's green eyes crinkled at the edges as he gave a welcoming nod. He was around the same height as Eric, with a leaner build. Still, he was no slouch in the muscle department.

"And this is Desmond Phillips, or Des," Avery said as he offered a warm smile.

Des had a sharp blue gaze. His muscular, stocky build was a few inches shorter and a few pounds heavier than Sin's. His buzz cut was a dark blond that made him appear tough, as if he could handle himself in a dark alley.

"Wanna see my frogs?" Andy asked Amelia, drawing Simone's attention.

"Heck yes." Amelia, a tomboy at heart, glanced at Simone for permission.

Frogs, bugs, and snakes fascinated her, much to Simone's disgust. The child hadn't inherited the love of all things creepy and crawly from her. Simone nodded, and both kids scampered up the circular staircase.

Avery watched them go, then refocused on Simone and her mom. "Would you like a tour?"

"Is the pope Catholic?" Lorraine blurted before Simone could politely refuse. She bit back a laugh, thankful for her mom's enthusiasm. She was dying to see the house too, but didn't want to appear nosy.

"Can I tag along?"

They all turned toward the voice as woman who resembled Avery entered the foyer. Avery introduced her as Terry, Des's wife, who also happened to be Avery's sister.

Standing side by side, it was obvious the two were sisters. Yet,

Avery had a softness in her features that Terry didn't have, and her hair was more auburn than Terry's brown hair. Both had brown eyes and the same slender build, but again, Avery's was softer with more curves. Terry's body was more defined, as if she worked out.

"I can't resist her tours. It's where I get most of my decorating ideas." Terry gave Avery a hip bump after Avery had led them into a huge living room that belonged on the cover of *House Beautiful.*

"Oh my." Lorraine looked around, awe evident in her expression. "You have to give me your decorator's name."

Avery stood taller and a pleased smile lit her face. "I did it all myself." Her tone held pride. "Putting the things I love together is a hobby."

"You definitely have a knack for it."

Simone nodded. "I agree with Mom."

As gorgeous as it was, the space also looked lived in. A laptop lay next to a TV remote on the coffee table. Books were strewn about, along with a few magazines. The room opened up to a gourmet kitchen, which featured state-of-the-art-appliances and natural stone countertops. Golds and yellows of the walls blended with greens and blues in the upholstery.

"I love the colors and the hardwood floors," she added.

"Wait until you see the master bedroom," Terry whispered conspiratorially. "It's to die for."

Grinning, Simone followed her mother, Terry, and Avery up the curved staircase as one thought struck. Her entire condo could fit into the entrance alone.

As predicted, Avery's bedroom was worth the trip. A dark hardwood four-poster bed was the centerpiece. Various shades of blue graced the bedspread, pillows, and window treatments. Anyone would have sweet dreams after falling asleep in this room.

All the other rooms were just as put together. Blue was definitely a unifying color throughout the home's decor.

"I've seen pictures of glorious bathrooms." Lorraine lovingly touched the coppery bronze faucet. "But I've never been this close and personal to one so beautiful." She glanced at Avery. "I love those tiles."

Simone figured tiles like those had to come from some exotic place, but Avery confessed she found them at the local building supply warehouse. "And they were on sale, to boot," she added.

When they exited the final room, Avery pointed toward the staircase. "Let's go find the others, shall we?"

The group retraced their steps to the living room where the men waited.

A bit of envy tugged at Simone as she watched how solicitous the two married men were toward their wives. Sin had a proprietary arm around Avery as little glances flitted back and forth between them. Des and Terry had their own way of flirting. For one thing, Des's gaze never left his wife for long. Too many times in the few moments they stood talking, the two would grin as if sharing some little joke.

"Damn!" Eric harrumphed. "Can we just get through an evening where I don't have to feel like I'm in a Hallmark movie?" he asked, proving she was obviously not the only one to notice. He did an exaggerated eye roll and headed out to the deck that overlooked a lake.

"Don't mind him," Des said in a teasing tone. "He's just jealous because he can't seem to find anyone who'll put up with him." Des then looked straight at Simone and his smile grew. "Or maybe not. After all, he's never brought a date to these get-togethers before, and he's the one who arranged tonight's."

A spotlight couldn't have done more to point out Simone as everyone in the room, including Lorraine, turned their assessing glances her way.

The chiming doorbell saved her from further embarrassment.

Seconds later, Scotty and a woman who looked a lot like a female Eric walked in. She had to be related to him. Intrigued, Simone approached the newcomers as Scotty introduced her as Trish, Eric's sister.

"Where's Eric?" Trish asked.

"He's outside. I asked him to start the barbecue," Sin said, shaking her hand.

Simone smiled and offered, "I'll go and bring him back inside."

"I'll go with you," Trish said as she followed her out the door.

Eric had finished setting up the barbecue and now leaned

against the deck railing with his back to them. Arms bent at the elbow and forearms resting on the rail, he stared out at the vast wilderness that was Sin and Avery's backyard.

The noise of her sliding the screen door shut drew his attention and he spun around.

His warm gaze met hers, then it chilled slightly and closed altogether when he noticed Trish.

"You don't mind that I tagged along," Trish asked in a cautious voice.

Realizing the awkward moment, Simone hung back. When they were side by side, Trish and Eric's resemblance was even more striking. Simone didn't catch all that went on between them, but eventually Eric smiled and hugged Trish.

Trish turned toward her. As she stepped past Simone to open the screen door, she gave Simone a relieved smile. "That went better than I'd hoped," she said before heading inside.

Simone refocused on Eric, whose eyes were once again filled with warmth. She strolled toward him. The entire time, their gazes were locked.

Halting a foot in front of him, she continued meeting his stare. His eyes, as dark as night, held promise. All kinds of pinging sped throughout her system. No matter how he looked at her, the excitement he elicited seemed to always be there, close to the surface and ready to explode. This was all new to Simone and she honestly didn't know quite how to handle it without doing something stupid to give away her inexperience.

"What do you think of my friends?" His smile quelled her nerves and drew her in.

She offered one in return. "They're nice."

"Nice? Ouch." His smile turned more teasing. "You're not just being polite, are you?"

"Of course not, silly." She reached out and slid her arm through his. "You need to quit hiding and come inside." About to start for the house, she paused and peered at him with a playful grin. "Unless you'd rather the party came out here." She glanced around. "It's definitely a beautiful spot."

He bent to nuzzle her neck. "I'd rather stay out here and keep you all to myself tonight."

As if on cue, the patio screen door opened and Des stepped out. "Hey, you two. The party's inside." His gaze swept the area, clearly noting what she and Eric had already discovered.

He leaned inside the door. "It's gorgeous out here."

"What'll you have, Simone?" Sin asked, coming up to them and handing Eric a beer. "That's from a new brewery I found. Try it and tell me what you think."

Eric took a swig and shrugged. "It's okay."

Sin scoffed. "Just okay?"

As she gave Sin her drink order, Des joined them.

"Don't listen to him." Des grunted. "The beer is damn good. He's just pissed because we ruined his party of two."

When Eric glanced at her with an apologetic expression, Simone laughed. "I'm actually glad you brought the party out here. It's too beautiful an evening to be inside." No matter that the outside, as well as the inside, was grander than anything Simone was used to.

"Hey, Andy, you wanna throw the football?" Des asked when Andy and Amelia burst out through the patio door, obviously done with looking at his frogs.

"Sure." Andy glanced at Amelia. "You wanna play too?"

Des waved. "Come on. It's just catch. No tackling or roughhousing tonight."

Amelia didn't need to be asked again. Yep, that was her daughter. It did Simone's heart good to see her laughing and running around without a care in the world. To be pulled into this wonderful fold of good-natured friends along with her daughter? A mother couldn't ask for anything more.

Why had she turned Eric down all those years ago?

Simone kept stealing surreptitious glances at him, trying to answer that very question. Fifteen minutes of silent observation later as he cooked burgers and hot dogs on the grill, she still had no ready answer.

Life was sure funny. If she'd given Eric the time of day back in high school, she might have had a different outcome. But then she wouldn't have Amelia. Simone would never give her up for anything, so maybe that was the way of things. They came full circle.

"Food's all out on the table, buffet style, so have at it when you're ready," Avery called out to those playing football.

Every now and then, Simone glanced at her mother. She finally gave up worrying about whether Lorraine was having a good time after continually seeing that she'd made ready friends with the moms, both Avery's and Des's, who'd arrived soon after Scotty and Trish. That was a plus she hadn't expected.

Simone dished out potato salad, added it to the burger and fruit salad already on her plate, and took a seat at the table next to Eric.

When the impromptu football game finally ended, the players, including Amelia, took turns piling food on their plates before joining them at the table.

Sin disappeared inside for a moment while they were finishing eating, and fast, upbeat music filtered out from inside the house. Terry jumped up from the table and pulled Des to the middle of the deck, where he spun her into the beginnings of a swing dance, and Sin and Avery quickly joined them with their own version of fast dancing. A few minutes later, Scotty convinced Trish to give it a go.

Eric wiped his hands on his napkin and grabbed Simone's hand when he noticed her tapping her foot to the beat. "Come on. They're playing our song."

"I didn't know we had a song." Not only that, the music died the moment she stood.

"We do now." His dimples made a bigger appearance than usual, and Simone couldn't help but be flattered by his attention.

Another song, this one a love ballad, began playing by the time Eric wrapped her in his arms. Mesmerized by the slow beat, Simone swayed back and forth with him in some kind of crazy mating ritual, feeling as if she'd died and gone to heaven. She already was half in love with him, so it was only a matter of time before making love. The idea thrilled her, especially when she realized how well they fit together during the dance.

When the song eventually ended, Eric leaned close and whispered, "We'll finish this later. I promise."

She simply offered her warmest smile as an answer, unable to articulate how much she anticipated *later*.

After the sun had dipped into the horizon, Sin lit a blaze in the copper fire pit on the deck. Thankful the party wasn't ending just yet, Simone sat in a circle with the others in canvas folding chairs Avery had brought out earlier.

"So did you ever find out if the black pickup was following you?" Andy asked Amelia after a lull in the conversation, loud enough for Simone to overhear.

Simone froze for a second and stared dumbfounded at her daughter. "You saw a black pickup?"

Shrugging, Amelia glanced down and fiddled with her shoelace. "I dunno." Then she peered over at Scotty, who suddenly appeared to be very interested in the landscape, even though it was too dark to see much past the fire's flames.

Eric cleared his throat. In the firelight, she was close enough to see that his expression said he knew all about it.

"What the hell is going on, and why haven't you told me?" Simone glared at Eric, who held up his hands.

"Don't look at me. It was all their doing." His nod indicated Scotty and Trish.

"We didn't want to worry you until we had something concrete," Scotty said, which did nothing to allay her fears.

"I followed him," Trish chimed in.

"And?" Simone's expectant gaze went from Trish to Scotty and back again.

"We're not sure."

"I wish you had mentioned it." Simone directed the comment to her daughter. She then refocused on Scotty and Trish. "I've been seeing a black pickup for weeks now. What if it's the same one who tried to run us off the road the day of Amelia's abduction attempt?"

The very idea scared the bejeebers out of her. Maybe it was time to go to the police. Yet, she had no proof. And what if the sightings were coincidental?

"Tell us about that day," Sin urged her.

After Simone did as he asked, the discussion turned to the possibility of the stalker following Amelia to camp where Scotty or

126

Eric wouldn't be around to save her in the event of another attempt. Why they felt there might be, she had no idea. Nevertheless, the notion lurked inside her subconscious, and she said as much.

"Amelia can spend the night here," Avery offered. "If you're worried about her safety."

"Oh please, Mom? Andy is the coolest. That way we can finish playing World of Warcraft."

They spent a few minutes discussing the pros and cons of her daughter spending the night. The house was like a fortress and had security cameras around the perimeter. If Simone hadn't been swayed by that, Amelia's enthusiasm for the solution sealed the deal.

"Okay, but don't stay up too late." Simone smiled, not wanting to show her worry. "You don't want to be tired on your first day of camp."

"I'll be fine, Mom. Thanks." Amelia jumped up from the folding chair and gave her a quick hug before following Andy into the house.

"I really appreciate it," Simone said, turning back to Avery and Sin.

Staying made her daughter happy while keeping her safe at the same time. That way, the pickup posed no threat. At least, not to Amelia.

Lorraine glanced at her watch. "I don't know about you all, but I'm an early riser, which means it's way past my bedtime."

"I'll make sure Simone gets home," Eric said when Lorraine's gaze landed on Simone.

"I'll keep an eye out for black pickups," Simone assured her mother. "If I see any, I'll call you."

Eric shook his head. "If you see one, it's time to bring in the police."

His comment eased her mind. These men seemed to know how to deal with would-be stalkers. Thank God she'd met Eric and his friends. She never realized how vulnerable she'd been living alone with no family around for all those years.

"We're ready to head out too." Scotty stood and began folding his chair. He helped Trish with her chair, then set both against the house.

Trish said her good-byes and hugged Eric. "I'm going to see Dad tomorrow, if you'd like to go with me."

Eric nodded. "Sure. What time?"

They made arrangements to meet in the morning around ten.

"How about a game of cards?"

Simone, along with the others agreed with Des's suggestion and the small group headed for the house.

Following Eric, she was amazed by how comfortable she felt with them and how much she'd missed by not having friends. Oh, she had acquaintances, but she'd never been able to drop her reserve with them. She'd missed out on so much, and so had Amelia.

But no more.

<><><>

ALL TOO soon, it was time to go. She'd kissed Amelia good-bye over an hour earlier, confident she would be safe in Sin and Avery's house. Eric's partners were take-charge kind of men, just like him. Her mom had texted to say no one had followed her home, which was a big relief.

"Thanks so much for a wonderful evening." Simone already viewed these two couples were friends. In fact, she definitely wanted to spend more time with them. Hopefully sooner rather than later.

They were fun. Simone realized that after her experience at that frat party in college, she'd become mistrustful of people in general and had pretty much shut herself off from making friends. That aspect of her life had already begun to change, thanks to the man she followed out to his car.

As Eric helped her inside, the thought warmed her more than a little bit.

CHAPTER SIXTEEN

WHEN A key turning in the lock alerted him, Michael quickly hid behind the bedroom door. Snake-like tension curled inside his belly as he readied for the perfect opportunity to strike. He'd anticipated this moment for hours.

"I had a great time tonight," a male voice said.

Michael frowned. Was the guy a date?

"It doesn't have to end here." He recognized Simone's voice. "Amelia's safe and sound. I don't have to pick her up until noon. Would you like a nightcap?"

"I thought you'd never ask."

Where in the hell was the kid? She was always with the mom. Was she at Grandma's? Michael hadn't expected that. He couldn't very well complete the job without the brat.

He damn sure hadn't expected Simone to invite some guy back to her place. That was so unlike the lady. She'd come across as one uptight bitch in those few lunches they'd shared. When had her MO changed, and why hadn't he realized it?

Michael crouched behind a door and watched between the crack as Simone opened a bottle of wine. For over twenty minutes, he waited for the guy to leave.

When the couple began smooching on the couch, he realized his predicament. Once they headed for the bedroom to finish what they'd started, the gig would be up.

Glancing at the patio door, he sighed in resignation at the only path available.

<><><>

ERIC FROZE. A bucket of ice water couldn't have dampened his ardor more than the sound of a sliding screen door opening, then closing, coming from the master bedroom. He broke the kiss and glanced in that direction, not sure if he'd imagined the noise or not. Still, remembering everyone's concern about someone possibly following Amelia, he shot off the sofa.

"What's the matter?"

Ignoring Simone's shocked question, he ran toward the living room balcony. Once there, Eric leaned over the railing but only caught shadows moving on the ground below. Brushing past Simone, he hurried to the master bedroom and stepped into the room. The drapes framing the sliding door to the bedroom balcony moved slightly in the breeze and he stepped past them, peering over the railing to search the ground beneath the bedroom balcony as well.

Simone met him at the door. "What's going on?"

"Did you leave your balcony slider open?"

"Yes. I'm on the third floor. I like fresh air and it's so nice out." She peered at him in the darkness. "Why?"

Eric shook his head and glanced behind him to search the black night. "I thought I heard something."

"It's a long drop and not an easy climb. Still, I'm glad Amelia is staying with Sin and Avery." She gave him a wry smile. "Ordinarily, I wouldn't dream of leaving my daughter with strangers. But she was having such a good time with Andy that I hated to say no. It's been a lonely summer for her after having to leave friends behind when I moved back home."

"I'm glad too. She couldn't be in better hands." Eric nodded and led Simone back inside through the bedroom. "I want to take a look around."

Shivering, she rubbed her arms, then wrapped them around her middle.

The urge to protect her surging through his system was an unaccustomed sensation. When nothing seemed out of the ordinary, he still wasn't happy.

"Pack some things. You're not staying here alone tonight."

MICHAEL SPED off down the street. He'd cut it too close. Who knew the lady would be entertaining a date? No matter; the man couldn't be around 24–7.

A siren sounded in the distance—a warning. He didn't dare tempt fate. She'd mentioned picking up her daughter tomorrow. He'd return in the morning to wait for another opportunity to take care of Simone and her kid once and for all. After he was done, no one would ever find them.

Then he could disappear and move on to the next job.

CHAPTER SEVENTEEN

ERIC GLANCED at the hallway Simone had just disappeared through, fully intending to take things slow. He certainly never meant to spend the night with her, yet she had appeared too relieved at his order to pack a bag before rushing out of the room to do his bidding.

Now he had no choice. Protecting her was all encompassing. He'd just have to keep his hands to himself. After all, he wanted a lifetime with her. It was much too early in their relationship to consummate their relationship, no matter how badly he wanted to. Though the thought of waiting any longer was torturous, he could wait.

Simone returned with an overnight bag. "I really appreciate your offer."

"I care about you, Simone," he answered, taking the bag and leading her out the door. As she stopped to lock it, he added, "I'm damn sure planning on keeping you safe."

"I'll admit I do feel safe and sound with you." She smiled. Not the brilliant one he was used to seeing, but it was still a smile nonetheless. "The more I'm with you, the more the guy in the pickup seems less of a threat."

"Good. I don't like seeing you upset."

"Being with you is a definite plus."

When she kissed his cheek, he wanted to howl at the moon or pound his chest. He loved hearing the approval in her voice. Simone trusted him, and he'd never betray that trust.

Once he had her ensconced in his condo, she glanced around. "Wow. This looks a lot different from my unit."

"My decorator got carried away." Eric flashed a self-deprecating smile to cover his embarrassment.

"Now I see the similarities."

"Similarities?"

She nodded. "This is what I'd expect from someone who's friends with Sin and Avery." She fingered the woodwork, clearly admiring the workmanship. "Your decorator knew her stuff."

"She should have. I paid her enough."

"I'm sure you did." Simone walked farther into the room like a queen reigning over her castle, which in this case happened to be his castle. No matter. Given time, it would be hers. The thought warmed him. He rather liked the analogy.

He cleared his throat and wiped his palms on his jeans, surprised to realize they were actually sweaty. "Let me show you the guest room." He picked up her bag, but before he'd taken two steps, she stopped him with, "Why can't I stay with you?"

He mulled her question around in his thick-skulled brain, trying to remember why. Then it hit him. She wasn't a one-night stand. She was long term. And nothing in his being would change his mind about that.

Until she came up behind him and wrapped her arms around him. Then she stood on tiptoe, pulling him closer.

She kissed his neck. Working her way to his ear, she took a nip and whispered invitingly, "Please?"

Christ almighty. He practically embarrassed himself right on the spot. He gripped her wrist, stilling her movements. "What're you doing?"

Pink flared on her cheeks as she straightened and wouldn't meet his gaze. "Nothing."

Her answer drew his frown. "It wasn't nothing, and you know it."

She licked her lips and then pressed them together, her brows also drawing in. "I just thought we were on the same wavelength." Her gaze flew to a spot behind him, obviously still unable to look him in the eye. "Obviously, I was wrong."

Damn, he'd embarrassed her. However, her forwardness had reminded him of those girls in high school, and his instinctive jump to anger had erupted so quickly, he hadn't been able to contain it. His emotions were in a jumble, his past insecurities leading the pack and making him a total basket case.

Simone had seemed so genuine and real. Unfortunately, Eric had thought that about his last date. Yep. He was losing his hold on reality. Simone was different. She had to be.

Unused to opening up, he had no idea how to relay his fears, but he had to try. "I need to explain what just happened."

Still gripping her wrist, he tugged and led her to his sofa. Looking up at him in confusion, she sat down at his insistence, but he remained standing.

Eric doubted Simone was on the make, like all those women before her, but he had to be sure. So he paced, struggling for a way to begin. Finally, he decided on the truth.

"I'm done with one-night stands. I want a relationship. With you. If that's not what you want, then—" He shrugged. "I'll have to pass."

As much as he fought to remain calm, his tone came out a little harsh. He prayed that she wasn't one of those who just wanted a good time. It messed with his mind to think he could have read her all wrong.

"I . . . I don't know what to say other than I want the same." Simone jumped up and hurried to him, peering up at him with a loving gaze. "I'm not sure what to do in these situations. My one and only experience at sex was after being drugged. I don't remember much."

She was drugged? "Shit."

Eric struggled to take her bombshell in stride, a huge feat considering he'd just been blown away. Not only that, he felt like a total jerk for jumping to conclusions, making him someone not worthy of shining her shoes. *As usual.* The news definitely trumped his insecurities by a mile.

Wait . . . did she say her one and only time?

"I didn't know," he choked out.

Once again, she wouldn't meet his gaze. "Nobody does. Except me and those involved." She went over to his sofa, sat down, and continued staring straight ahead, looking as forlorn as if she'd lost her best friend.

Unable to think of anything to do except join her, he did just that. "You want to talk about it?" In an effort to comfort her, Eric wrapped an arm around her. She deserved so much more, but it was all he had to offer at the moment.

Simone sniffled, and he glanced at her. Tears trekked down her face as if a damn had burst inside her.

Eric hated seeing women cry, especially one he cared about. He pulled her closer and kissed each side of her face, wiping away some of her tears with the pad of his thumb. That only increased her sobbing. Without knowing what else to do, he just held her.

"That's it," he murmured against her hair. "Get it all out."

They stayed like this for what seemed like hours, but only minutes had passed since her sniffles slowed to one every so often. He checked her face to see her tears had dried. Her eyes were closed, but as if sensing his gaze, she opened them and offered him a wan semblance of a smile. Again, not the one he loved, but it was still a smile.

"I never cried when it happened."

"Tell me about it."

COMPASSION SHONE in Eric's eyes. And because of his reaction, opening up to him about her secret wasn't as daunting as Simone had once feared. If the idea revolted him, she'd rather know now, before she got any more involved with him.

"I was a college freshman. Blaine an upperclassman. We dated a few weeks. I thought the sun rose and set on him. Then he took me to a frat party and my world turned upside down. I woke up back in my dorm, sore, with bloody underwear and no memory of how I got there or what happened after I drank a cola Blaine had given me. The night is still a blurry haze of images. Imagine my surprise when I realized several weeks later that I was pregnant."

"Wow! That's beyond shitty." He stared at her with wide eyes before his expression softened. "Did you go to the police?"

"No. It was my word against his. I'd read about the Kennedy trial for a class I was taking. Justice in this country is for those who can afford a good lawyer. I couldn't. My dad had died a few years earlier, leaving my mom with huge medical bills that used up most of the life insurance, so funds were tight. I was going to Georgetown on a scholarship."

Simone sniffled once more. "Besides, Mom had finally gotten over Dad's death. By then, she was planning a wedding and starting a new life. I couldn't risk ruining her happiness, so I took their hush money and made plans to get my education at another school. When I realized I was pregnant, I confronted Blaine again. He denied everything, said I was delusional. And since I couldn't remember exactly what happened, I accepted it. I was too intimidated to do anything other than ask for more money. At that point, all I wanted was his signature waiving all rights to my baby. His parents gladly added more money to the pot in order to get rid of me."

She shrugged and added, "They wanted me to have an abortion. I let them think that's what I'd do. Then I left town, took another scholarship I was offered, and the rest is history."

Simone risked glancing at him to gauge his reaction. "You're the only person I've ever told about Amelia. It was tough, mainly because I was all alone."

"I always thought you were perfect. You should have had the perfect life, but that was stolen from you."

"It may not be perfect, but I wouldn't trade Amelia for anything."

Eric's earlier actions came to mind, and she couldn't let it drop. He'd been angry and she wanted to know why.

After another short pause, she prodded, "Your turn."

"What do you mean, my turn?"

Simone snuggled deeper into Eric's warmth. His strong arms felt wonderful and his nonjudgmental listening had done much to lift her spirits. The pain was still there, but the blister had popped. Crying over it had been cathartic. Opening up about it had cleaned the wound and now it could heal.

"I'm curious," she said, finally drawing up enough courage to ask. "Why were you so upset when I wanted to sleep in your room?" In her limited experience, it didn't seem normal.

It was his turn to find a spot on the wall until she gripped his chin and forced him to meet her gaze. "I told you my deepest secret. Now I want to hear yours."

"How do you know I have a secret?"

"Are you telling me you don't?"

"No. But once you hear my mine, you may decide your earlier opinion back in high school was right on. My past isn't pretty."

"I doubt it." When he remained silent, she said, "What can be worse than rape?"

"Okay. You've made your point." His quick laugh sounded forced. "I just need a minute to figure out how to spill my guts."

"Take all the time you need. We have all night."

After another long pause, Eric began speaking. "I already mentioned that I didn't have the best parenting. My childhood was pretty awful."

He spent a little time explaining about his parents' abuse and neglect before moving on to tell Simone about his older sister, how he'd looked up to Trish until she stole the money he'd saved for college.

"That's why I went into the Air Force. To be truthful, it was probably a good thing. High school wasn't easy. Definitely not fun and games." He broke off, as if gathering courage to continue.

Simone reached for his hand and gave it a reassuring squeeze. "Go on. I'd really like to know more about you."

He glanced up at her. Sadness filled his eyes, but she also caught a hint of guilt and shame in those brown depths.

"I won't judge. I promise."

"Like I said, school was hard. I'm dyslexic. Reading was and is extremely difficult for me. Words jump all over the page. Thankfully, I'm a whiz at memorization."

"That's not a crime. It's not even close to being a deep dark secret."

"It is when you sleep with the girls who help you get by in school."

"Wow. That's . . ."

"Go ahead; spit it out. It's prostitution. Plain and simple."

"I wasn't going to say that. I meant to say that's sad."

"Sugarcoat it any way you want. The truth is I became my lying, cheating mother who'd turn a trick for a fix." He snorted. His expression turned from pained to disgusted in a heartbeat. "You were right not to go out with me. I was scum of the earth."

"Wait a minute." She held up a hand. "You can't call yourself scum when it takes two to have sex. What kind of person would use you like that?"

"Shallow ones. Just like me. Just like I've been my entire life. I wanted us to be different, so when you came on to me like you did, I took it wrong."

"I'm sorry, Eric. I didn't know."

"Like you said earlier. No one does but those involved."

"So, let me get this straight. You're dyslexic, and you used sex to get help?" She wrapped her head around his struggle, yet from her vantage point he was the opposite of scum. It only made him more vulnerable. And lovable. "Didn't you feel used at the time?"

"Of course not. I enjoyed it. Every orgasm." He threw out a harsh laugh. "Pretty ugly, huh?"

Simone shook her head. "You used what was available at the time. If you were still doing it, I might be concerned."

"That's just it. I've never had a meaningful relationship." He exhaled and put his face in his hands. "At least now you know." He gave her a wry look from between his fingers. "Told you it wasn't pretty."

"True. But I understand your motives. You were a kid without any parental support, trying to better yourself."

"Funny, I never thought of it like that. I've never felt the urge to talk to anyone about those years, other than my closest friends. I certainly haven't told anyone except Scotty about the girls who traded sex with me to help me with my homework."

"Trust me. Talking helps. At least, it helped me." She stared off into space, continuing to absorb what he'd just revealed. Refocusing on him, she said, "You mentioned never having a meaningful relationship. What about us?"

"To be honest, I've never wanted one. Until now."

His gaze was so earnest, she couldn't help but lean in with the intention of kissing him. She stopped short, her lips an inch from his. "I'm dying to kiss you, but I don't want you to get the wrong idea."

He eyed her lips, his grin turning wicked. "And what idea is that?"

"That I want your body. I do. But I must warn you, I want a whole lot more."

"Really." His lips grazed hers. Once. Twice. Then again. "What do you want in return?"

"Nothing but your love."

"And what do I get?"

"My love," she said in a fervent tone. "I hope that's enough."

"It's a great start," he whispered before his mouth closed the small gap.

Like a bee to honey, she was drawn into the kiss's sweetness. Eventually their kisses grew hungrier, hotter, as desire flared within her and grew. The touch of his lips became explosive.

Simone definitely wanted more. She wanted to feel him inside her. For the first time in her life, she wanted to love a man and *feel* his love in return. Yet this was still so new to her, so she let Eric show her by example.

Sometime while they'd kissed, he'd gently maneuvered them until they were lying on the couch with him on top of her. How it happened, Simone had no idea. All she knew was she'd found heaven as Eric nestled into that perfect spot. The contact was electric. She could stay like this forever; it felt that good.

His mouth continued its onslaught as wave after wave of sensation rolled over her—waves lapping at her center, going higher and higher. Simone moaned his name, then added breathlessly, "Make love to me."

"Thought you'd never ask." Taking his time, Eric removed her blouse and undid her bra, releasing her breasts. He spent long moments just suckling.

The pleasure built. So much so, she swore she would die from it.

He sat upright and snared her gaze.

In slow motion he took off his shirt, watching her watch him the entire time—an immensely erotic moment. He then stood to unzip his pants. As he pushed them down, his gaze never faltered, even when his erection sprang to life, extending the tension.

He continued eying her like she was the most beautiful woman in the world.

Though slightly nervous now that their lips weren't joined, she felt beautiful. And sexy.

Simone concentrated on his steady gaze. Those warm bedroom eyes quelled the worst of her fears as he slowly undid her zipper. Keeping to his unhurried rhythm, he eased her jeans off her legs.

"Now that we've dispensed with all obstacles, we can take our time," he whispered in a voice full of promise. In a reverent motion, he slid his hands up and down her body, drawing delicious shivers that started from within and spread out to her extremities.

Still eying her with an intensity that took her breath away, he lowered himself above her. Now naked with no barriers between them other than the condom he'd donned just moments ago, she reveled in the feel of him. All sinewy muscles and strength.

She sensed he was holding himself back while at the same time allowing her to adjust to his weight and size. If she hadn't loved him before this, that alone would have sent her over the edge.

His lips grazed hers again before he took full possession of her mouth, Eric drew out her moans, one deep kiss after another, and then he was inside her, moving in slow strokes. It was all she could do to hold on to the pleasure as it peaked.

Why had she waited so long to feel these wonderful sensations?

The thought was lost as he swept her away, demanding she stay with him.

<><><>

SIMONE AWOKE, reveling in the warmth of the sun on her face

coming in from the balcony window. She stretched, noting a little soreness from the night before.

Happiness engulfed her as she peeked at Eric. Eyes closed in slumber, he appeared peaceful . . . and vulnerable. He'd given her a precious gift, one she'd remember the rest of her life. Gently, so as not to wake him, she slid out from the covers, but his hand on her arm stopped her movement.

"Where are you going?"

Heat streaked from her neck to her cheeks. It seemed silly to be embarrassed after all they'd done the night before, but still, she wasn't used to his intense gaze this early in the morning. Heck, waking up in a man's bed took some getting used to.

"To the bathroom." If only to brush her teeth. She darn sure wasn't going to kiss him with morning breath.

"Mind if I shower with you?"

His sinful gaze added more flames to her cheeks. The idea of showering with him left her off-kilter, as if the world had tilted on its axis.

"No, I'd love it." Lordy, who knew a month ago she'd be this free and easy with any man?

"I'm going to see my father with Scotty and Trish. Scotty's driving. He's picking me up in half an hour, so I don't have time to finish anything we start."

Still, he found time to give her one more orgasm while soaping up, leaving her in a sensual haze as he dressed.

Simone rinsed, turned off the faucet, then dried herself off, dressing while Eric shaved. Running the electric razor over his face, he watched her from the mirror. His heated gaze sent funny tingles to her insides. She could get used to this.

When they were both dressed, they moved to the kitchen for coffee. Eric pulled out a couple of bowls and several boxes of cereal for her to choose from.

"I shouldn't be much more than a few hours," he said while rooting for the milk in the fridge.

"If I'm not here, I'll be picking up Amelia to get her to tennis camp."

They ate in companionable silence as if they'd done it for years.

Simone could get used to this too.

Her spirits nose-dived when the doorbell rang. She definitely wasn't used to emotional ups and downs when it came to men. Jeez, how sappy could she be? He was only going to see his sick father, which wouldn't take long.

Eric kissed her full on the lips. "I'll see you soon." Then he was out the door.

Simone stared at the empty space, already missing him, but thanking God for her newfound happiness. She heaved a contented sigh, then grabbed the remote, intending to pass the time watching a movie.

For the first time in ages, since well before Amelia's kidnapping attempt, she felt safe. Eric's love gave her that.

CHAPTER EIGHTEEN

"ARE YOU ready?"

Question of the year, Eric thought as he sprinted down the flight of stairs with Scotty, Trish by his side, both appearing as if they were going on a picnic.

"As ready as I'll ever be."

This was no picnic. Or maybe it was—if the picnic included fire ants, rain, and sand in the food. Visiting his father was definitely the first thing on his don't-do list. Having his eye pierced with a hot poker was a close second.

As they neared the car, Trish stopped to wrap her arms around him, offering him a hug of encouragement. Unused to displays of affection, Eric flinched for a second, until the grudge he'd held on to for so long disintegrated. An embarrassed flush heated his cheekbones.

The sensation snaked around his heart and filled him with a warmth that had long been missing from his life. One full of acceptance. That he'd also received acceptance from Simone added to his sense of well-being.

Given his reaction, his soul had obviously craved affection. Craved love from someone he'd thought of as a mother figure. Kind of sick to realize after all these years, but Eric was tired of living with negative emotions. Starting right now, he intended to focus only on the positive.

Still, as much as he wanted to pretend a warm-and-fuzzy family reunion awaited him, there was no way to spin his existing father-son relationship into a positive.

"I'm so glad you've decided to do this," Trish said, breaking into his thoughts and boosting his lagging resolve with another hug.

"Yeah, well . . ." He didn't know what else to say. Definitely not the truth. That he was hoping for some kind of miracle. That by some divine goodness, his father would actually give a flying fig and appreciate the effort. "I don't expect much."

"Neither did I. At first." Her smile turned rueful. "But the encounter changed my life. Not for Dad, but for me. I let go of the anger, the disappointment, and the hurt. I cried for the little girl who wanted a nurturing, loving father and ended up with him instead. I deserved better. And so did you. We didn't get a fair deal with our dad. We both know life isn't fair. Bottom line? He just never should have had children."

"Don't worry. I've got your back," Scotty interjected, clicking the locks on his car.

Reaching for the door handle, Eric nodded. His gaze traveled from Scotty to Trish, then to the building behind him, where he'd left Simone. Life sure did have a few ups and downs. He'd lived with the downs most of his life, and now it was hard to believe he deserved the ups. But like Trish said, neither had gotten a fair deal with parents, so he prayed that he wouldn't blow it with Simone. She was a keeper.

Thoughts of the night before replayed in his head during the short drive to the hospital, providing the inspiration to stay upbeat.

As they walked into the marble reception area, Trish put her hand on Eric's shoulder. He stopped and glanced at her with eyebrows raised.

"I should warn you, seeing him won't be pretty. He's lost a lot of weight, and looks a hundred years old instead of fifty-nine."

Eric nodded. "Burning the candle at both ends will do that to anyone. And he had two wicks on each side."

"I'll wait down here," Scotty said as Trish pushed the elevator button.

As much as Trish had warned him, Eric wasn't prepared enough for the image before him when he entered the room. Dear old Dad had turned into an emaciated, wrinkled mess of a man. Tubes protruded from his nose, providing needed oxygen, and an IV needle in his arm fed him fluids from the overhanging bag.

His eyes opened, or rather one did. Where the second should have been, there was only a socket covered with skin. A toothless half smile formed.

"Eric? Is that you?"

Eric hid his stunned reaction behind a forced smile. "Hey, Dad." The last twelve years had taken a huge toll on Ronald Coleman.

"You've grown into a good-looking man." His father tried to sit up, but started wheezing and dropped back down. "Damn, I hate being this weak." He paused. "You look like you've done all right in spite of the bullshit I dealt you."

Eric swallowed hard, smoothing the lump that began forming. "I'm doing okay."

As he stared at his father, an interesting transformation took place, one he hadn't expected. The pure hatred he'd carried for his father for so long was rapidly being replaced by sadness for what might have been. Regret also made an appearance inside his mind's eye. Eric had spent so much time filled with negative emotions.

He was tired of being angry and full of bitterness. All for what? To what end? The pathetic man before him didn't deserve that much control over him.

To think he'd let Ronald Coleman run roughshod over his emotions all this time? Seeing the man now made him realize how useless and stupid it had been.

Trish had said all along that hatred and anger were wasted emotions. Eric aimed to redirect the energy to loving Simone and getting on with his life.

Eric couldn't pity his father. Ronald would despise the sentiment. His father was reaping what he'd sown. Still, empathy and compassion, also unexpected, filled Eric's heart to the brim. Though the man had been a worthless father, he was still a human being. At this point, Eric could easily be the bigger person. Hell, wasn't that his goal? To be the man Simone deserved?

"So . . ." He cleared his throat after an awkward silence. "How are they treating you?" he asked, for want of something to talk about. What else could he say?

"I get poked and prodded a lot," his father said on a wheeze. "It's my ticker. Can't do much. Even a walk to the bathroom 'bout does me in. I'm jonesing for a cigarette. They say I won't last long." He paused and closed his eye. "Which will be a blessing, since I can't smoke."

Eric wasn't certain if his father gone to sleep or not until the eye opened and Ronald stared straight at him with an earnest expression.

"I'm glad you're here. I shouldn't have done you so wrong." After another long wheeze, he added, "I was messed up. Nothing like dying to make a man look at his life and realize he has a few regrets."

The grim line of his mouth softened into a smile. "I lived what I knew. Trish's ma tried to help me until she decided I was a lost cause. Your ma tried to help me get clean before she got messed up too, thanks to me. We were two losers who shouldn't have had kids. I wish I could go back and undo the worst. Now, I have to face my maker. I wonder if he'll forgive me?"

Eric blinked, too choked up to speak right away. "I forgive you, Dad." He smiled, knowing it was the truth. "I'm sure the man upstairs will too."

"Thanks, boy. That eases my mind a little." He closed his eye.

A few minutes passed with no movement. Ronald had gone to sleep.

Eric used the sleeve of his shirt to wiped the moisture from his eyes before turning to Trish. "Thanks for urging me to do this."

She opened her arms. "You're welcome," she said as Eric stepped closer to her.

They hugged. For the first time in forever, Eric felt totally at peace. The anger guiding so much of his life entirely dissipated as realization set in. He'd not only forgiven his father and Trish, but he'd forgiven himself for being human.

Even more startling to discover was that what he felt extended to his mom, wherever she was. After hearing Ronald's admission about how she'd tried to help him and had gotten messed up in the process, Eric found that he could easily forgive Carrie Coleman for not being the mother he needed. He damned sure had never thought that was even remotely possible.

He sent up a silent prayer in hopes that she'd found help. Maybe it was time to look for her and see what he could do.

Eric hugged Trish tighter, knowing without a doubt that her words about forgiveness were right on. Having filled his heart with it, he was the true winner.

It felt wonderful to be so unencumbered. To be filled with hope, and the stirrings of familial love. After all, if Eric couldn't find his mom, his half sister would be the only blood family he would have left once his father's ticker finally gave out.

CHAPTER NINETEEN

SIMONE LEFT Eric's unit and started for her own condo. She still had to kill a couple of hours before picking up Amelia and taking her to camp, and it felt weird to spend them at Eric's place.

While unlocking the deadbolt, she felt a presence and glanced behind her. Startled to see someone coming toward her, she frowned.

"Michael? What are you doing here?"

"Hello, Simone." By now he was a few steps away. "I needed to speak to you."

Uneasiness set in and she quelled the desire to run. "How did you get my address?" She kept her voice modulated. After all, there was no reason to panic.

Until she saw his expression.

"You're coming with me." His smile didn't quite reach his eyes, as his nod indicated for her to go ahead of him.

"Why? What's going on?"

"Simple. We're going to pick up your daughter from wherever you stashed her."

Simone gaped at him, unable to fathom why he'd demand such a thing. Then everything fell into place at once in her mind—the easy way she'd met him, the coincidence that he was supposedly starting work the same day as she was, his unsolicited attention, the questions about her family and background. The strange inkling she'd had lately that something wasn't quite right with Michael had been dead-on. Could he possibly be her stalker?

Finding her wits, she shook her head. "No. I can't do that." There was no way she'd lead him to Amelia. Somehow she had to stall him until Eric and Scotty returned. She glanced at her watch.

"I thought you might resist." He pulled out a cell phone. "I don't like killing unless I get paid for it, but I will if finishing a job requires it." The expression in his eyes turned colder, if that were possible. "If you don't do what I say, all I have to do is call a number set to an incendiary device and your mother's house will no longer exist."

The devil himself couldn't have given a more sinister smile, which said more than words ever could. He enjoyed planting fear in the hearts of his victims. What's more, he clearly wasn't making idle threats.

"Get moving."

How had she not seen his true nature during those few lunch dates? Maybe her subconscious had, and that's why she'd no longer wanted to see him.

But the real question was: Who was paying him? The Moorecrofts? And why in the world would they want her dead? That was pretty extreme, even for people like them.

In slow motion, she started down the stairs with Michael right beside her. The entire time, her mind spun for ways to stall.

Simone couldn't forget his threat of harming her mother. Every now and again, she'd check to see if he still had the phone in his hand. That he did had her praying for a miracle.

As they reached the parking lot, Michael drew closer and reached his arm around her waist, making it appear as if they were a couple. She flinched, hating his touch. His cell phone dug into her back with their every step, reminding her of his intent. The hot, midday sun beat on her shoulders, yet fear kept her frozen.

Nearing the street, she spied the black truck parked along the side of the road, confirming her worst fears. She halted abruptly and pulled out of his grasp to glare up at him.

"You! You've been stalking us?"

"Not an easy task." He practically snarled the words.

"Why?" Her fear morphed into confusion. "What have we ever done to you?"

"It's nothing personal. It's business." He waved the cell phone. "Quit stalling and get moving."

About to follow his terse orders, Simone looked past his shoulder and caught a glimpse of a miracle. Something must have shown in her expression because Michael glanced behind him.

Taking advantage of the diversion, Simone snatched the cell phone from his hand and hurled it as far as she could.

"You bitch!" Michael backhanded her, sending her sprawling on the ground. Seeing stars and almost blacking out, she cringed, expecting more blows.

Scotty's car came to a screeching stop right in front of them, and Michael took off running.

Eric was out of the car in seconds. "Check on Simone," he yelled at Scotty before racing after Michael.

Tires squealed as the black pickup spun away from the curb. Unable to stop Michael's getaway, Eric rushed back to help Simone.

"Are you okay?"

"No," she said, trembling and taking deep calming breaths. She'd thought Michael was okay, but . . . "That man is crazy." How could she have not seen it? It brought back memories of those dark days before Amelia's birth when she lost faith in her judgment. "He demanded I take him to Amelia. There's no doubt in my mind he was going to kill us."

"I didn't get the plate number," Scotty said.

Her hands shaking, Simone brushed debris off her shorts. Remembering Michael's threat, she searched for his cell phone, which was still exactly where she'd thrown it, thank God.

"He said he was going to blow up my mom's house if I didn't do as he said." Simone held out the phone. "I need to warn her."

"Let me see that." Scotty took the phone and scanned through it.

"We need to notify the police." Eric pulled his phone out of his pocket at the same time Simone pulled her phone from her pocket and punched in her mother's number.

She hung up, relieved that her mom was playing it safe and leaving the premises.

After calling the police, Eric headed toward the street. Pointing to a blond wig and glasses discarded on the grass nearby, he shook his head. "We don't even know for sure what this guy looks like."

Seconds later, Eric was next to her. "You're still shaking." He wrapped an arm around her and kissed her temple as sirens sounded in the distance. "Don't worry, sweetheart. I won't let anything happen to you or Amelia." He pulled her into a bear hug. "I promise."

Simone sank into his warmth. The determination in his voice was calming. She believed him. Thank God that she'd allowed them into her life. Maybe she wasn't such a bad judge of character after all.

Scotty glanced at them. "The guy's threat has to be a bluff. There's only one number on this phone. More than a dozen calls have gone back and forth to it in the past few months, one just an hour ago."

While they waited for the police, Simone explained how she'd met Michael and had lunch with him a few times. Eric watched her closely as she spoke, but didn't comment.

Chaos reigned after several police cars came on the scene and policemen swarmed the area.

During that hour, Simone had spent most of it talking to Amelia by phone. Concerned for her safety, she was unwilling to think about what would have happened if her daughter hadn't spent the night with Sin and Avery.

She gave the heavens a quick glance, thanking the Lord for the way things turned out. Simone didn't have the heart to mention canceling her tennis camp over the phone. Amelia's excitement over going came out loud and clear. Michael, if that was his real name, didn't know where she was. He also couldn't know about the camp.

On the drive to Sin's house, a mental battle took place. One part of her wanted to hug her daughter and never let her go. The other part rationalized that Amelia would be safer at a camp, where no one knew where she was, than in her own home until the police figured out why a crazy man wanted to kill them.

Her fretting drew Eric's notice and he gave her leg a reassuring squeeze. "Remember my promise."

Overwhelmed with emotion, tears threatened to flow as Simone gave him a quick nod.

THE NEXT few hours flew by in a blur for Simone. She practically flew out of the car when Eric pulled into Sin's driveway, the desire to see Amelia her most fervent thought. The moment she saw her daughter, she pulled her into a bear hug.

"Mom, you're hurting me," Amelia said, trying to wiggle free.

Simone released her hold but still kept a protective hand on her shoulder. "Sorry. I just realized how much I'm going to miss you. Are you sure you want to go?"

The *are you nuts* look Amelia threw at her was priceless and something only a pre-teen could conjure up. "Yeah, I wanna go."

Simone finally resigned herself to letting her daughter go. Nothing would be gained from mentioning what had just happened, so she didn't say anything about it as she climbed into Eric's BMW. Still, she sat in the backseat next to Amelia, intending to hold her hand for the entire one-hour drive to the Virginia camp just outside of Charlottesville. Every time Amelia would try to pull her hand away, Simone only tightened her grip, ignoring her daughter's annoyed glare.

Thankfully, neither Simone nor Eric spotted any pickups, much less a black one on the road. In fact, for miles they encountered only a handful of cars.

After winding through the college town, vibrant and alive with activity, they drove another few miles to the camp's entrance where a guard stood sentry. Anyone entering the gate had to sign in before driving the last quarter of a mile to the compound. The camp's security eased Simone's worst fears of anything happening to her daughter.

Once Amelia was signed in, they found her room and Simone

helped her unpack. With nothing else use as a stalling tactic, Simone hugged her daughter, blinking back tears. This was the hardest thing she'd ever done. In their twelve years together, they'd never been separated for more than a night or two. Adding in all that had happened, Simone had to trust that God and the anonymity of the camp would take care of Amelia.

"I'll see you in two weeks, sweetie. Have fun." Simone let go and started for the parking lot where Eric waited, determined not to glance back and let Amelia see her tears or know of her hidden fears. Simone had lived with that emotion for too long, and she wasn't about to put something that heavy on her daughter's shoulders.

On the drive back, Eric's cell phone rang. He glanced at Simone. "It's Scotty." He put the call on speaker. "What's up?"

"Hey, guys," Scotty said. He then went on to relay what the police had discovered. As predicted, the bomb squad—after an extensive search of Lorraine's house—determined the threat a hoax.

"According to the police," Scotty continued, "the number in the guy's cell phone is registered to Blaine Moorecroft's political campaign. An aide reported it missing along with other items after a break-in several months ago. The theft's been documented." Simone and Eric glanced at each other as Scotty paused. "That's it so far. I'll keep you updated."

"Thanks, Scotty." Eric glanced at Simone. She could tell by his expression he was thinking the same thing she was.

Blaine Moorecroft was somehow involved in all of this. But why? That was her biggest question.

THANKFULLY, THE next few days were quiet. Simone had enjoyed the rest of the weekend with Eric as best she could, considering all that had happened.

She couldn't dismiss the idea that Blaine, or his family, was somehow responsible for sending Michael. Still, Simone couldn't accuse Blaine outright, but the fact that he was Amelia's father and had reasons not to want to broadcast that fact was just too coincidental for her liking.

Deep down, Simone couldn't dismiss his involvement. Her research on the Internet provided much information as to the why. Of course, she was cautious about revealing her suspicions, unwilling to do battle with the family without some kind of proof.

It had to be Blaine—or his dad. Maybe, since Blaine was running for a senate seat, he wouldn't want news of an out-of-wedlock daughter coming out to jeopardize his campaign.

When Simone voiced those thoughts to Eric on Sunday, he said, "Let the police handle the investigation. They'll be discreet, but thorough. More importantly, if it is the Moorecrofts, they won't try anything else now that everything is out in the open."

Simone nodded, praying that they would discover something tangible soon.

Just then her cell phone buzzed.

"Hi, sweetie," Simone said, answering Amelia's call.

"Today Coach Johnson spent an hour giving me some pointers," Amelia blurted before chattering excitedly about what a great time she was having.

As Simone listened to more of Amelia's adventures, she prayed the investigation would uncover something sooner rather than later.

CHAPTER TWENTY

B Y WEDNESDAY of the following week, it became clear to Simone that the investigation into why Michael was stalking her and her daughter had hit a brick wall. Apparently, he was a hired killer. The wig and glasses had provided enough DNA for a hit. The man was considered a phantom, responsible for over a dozen known deaths and most likely many more.

Because the cell phone had been reported stolen, the police had ruled out the Moorecrofts as suspects. This annoyed Simone, yet she understood the police department's position. The Moorecrofts were a powerful DC family. No one wanted to cross them unless they had solid evidence against them.

Still, she was happy to learn Eric's friends weren't hindered by the same constraints. The partners at SPC had promised to keep digging until they uncovered the full story about why someone wanted Simone and her daughter out of the picture. Like Simone, Eric knew of Blaine's past crime, and he wasn't about to dismiss the Moorecrofts so readily.

Midmorning on Thursday, Simone's office phone rang.

"Simone Harris speaking," she said upon answering it.

"Ms. Harris, this is Marilee Durant, Blaine Moorecroft's personal assistant."

Simone stiffened. Though the woman had a pleasant,

nonthreatening voice, her tone did nothing to ease Simone's trepidation over hearing Blaine's name mentioned.

About to tell the assistant she had nothing to say, Simone's overall fear quieted and her curiosity got the better of her. "Why are you calling?"

"Mr. Moorecroft would like a meeting to clear up the allegations that are floating about."

Simone smiled as amusement eclipsed the rest of her uneasiness. Of course he'd call them allegations. Well, Simone wasn't a naive teenager any longer. In fact, she no longer feared the Moorecroft name and relished the idea of seeing Blaine's face when she showed him a picture of her daughter and asked if he still had the audacity to deny raping Simone. The child was undoubtedly his.

"I agree. It *is* time to meet face-to-face." It was past time to put the episode behind her once and for all.

She wrote down the address, thankful that they were meeting in his office where the chances of him harming her there were nil— if he happened to be involved in hiring Michael. That was a matter for the police to figure out. Plus, the time coincided with her lunch hour.

After disconnecting, Simone called Eric to fill him in on the situation. When the call went to voice mail, rather than leave a message, she asked him to call her as soon as possible.

Before heading out, she scoured the Internet for information about Amelia's father. After checking several websites, one thing popped out at her. The attempt on Amelia had been made just weeks before Blaine Moorecroft's announcement of running for office.

Would his family attempt to kidnap her daughter to keep anyone from ever finding out the truth about her?

Simone wasn't sure. Could anyone be that cold-blooded? Of course, she wouldn't put anything past the senior Moorecroft if he thought a scandal could keep his precious son out of office. The more she thought about it, the more convinced she became that the father was behind it all. Now she really wanted to talk to Blaine to see what he knew.

Eric still hadn't returned her call by the time she left her office for the meeting. She tried one last time to reach him and when his voice mail picked up, she related everything that had transpired and what she was doing, including the assistant's name and number and the address of Blaine's office building.

"I was hoping you could accompany me. I'm heading there now. It would be great if you could meet me there, if you get this in time and if you're not too busy."

THE WALK to Blaine's office building took less time than expected. Peering up at the skyscraper, then glancing at the main entrance, Simone wondered how best to broach the meeting. What if they weren't behind the attempts?

She snorted, discarding the notion. These people were in it up to their eyeballs; she felt it in her blood. Emboldened by the thought, she stormed up to the double glass doors and inside, not stopping until she reached the elevator.

Simone pressed the button, resisting the urge to keep pushing. Having come this far, she started to doubt her rationale in making the trip. Before she could turn around and leave, the doors opened invitingly.

Oh, for heaven's sake. It was an office building. Nothing was going to happen to her. Still, she wished Eric had been able to join her.

After a quick trip to the fifteenth floor, she stepped out into a glass-and-granite waiting area. Holding her head high, she headed toward the only occupied desk.

The woman sitting behind it looked up at her approach. "Can I help you?"

"Yes. I'm here to see Blaine Moorecroft."

"Simone Harris, I presume?" When she nodded, the woman offered a satisfied smile. "Right on time. Mr. Moorecroft will appreciate your punctuality." She stood. "Right this way."

Simone followed the woman toward a corner office. The lady clearly wasn't any normal assistant, not in that designer getup. Simone might not be able to afford couture, but that didn't mean she didn't recognize it when she saw it draped on another woman.

"Go on in." The woman motioned after opening the door. "I'll alert him that you're here."

"Thanks," she murmured under her breath. "I think."

Simone entered the office, noting its opulence. *Must be nice to be rich.* Although, she wouldn't trade Amelia for any amount of money. As she waited, Simone stood gazing out one of the floor-to-ceiling windows, too distracted by her unsettled thoughts to enjoy the panoramic view.

The assistant poked her head in a moment later. "Mr. Moorecroft will be here shortly. Make yourself comfortable." Her nod indicated one of two chairs in front of a huge dark wood desk. "Can I get you some coffee or a soft drink? Or perhaps water?"

"Bottled water would be nice." Having walked in the midday heat, Simone was thirsty. She sat in the chair closest to the window.

Returning, the assistant said apologetically, "It's not cold."

"That's fine." Simone took the bottle and uncapped it as the assistant made a retreat.

Simone sipped from the bottle as she waited. The entire time, butterflies flapped inside her belly.

What was taking Blaine so long? Simone took another sip from the bottle and set it on the table beside her before she glanced at her watch.

The numbers blurred in front of her. She blinked, suddenly feeling clammy and hot. The effort to hold her head up became too much; she had to lean against the chair's back to steady herself. While taking deep breaths, the memory of when she'd last felt this way—the night Amelia was conceived—came back with startling clarity.

Now she grasped the situation more astutely. She'd been drugged. The assistant had drugged her. Why? On Blaine's orders?

Oh good Lord, what had she done?

Movement at the door drew her attention. The assistant, wearing a smirk that could only be called evil, stepped inside. "Good. You're under." She picked up the phone and said, "Blaine, I have someone in your office who is demanding to see you."

That didn't make sense. Simone recognized the fact even

through her haze of confusion. Blaine had asked her to come.

Please, Eric, hurry, she prayed, unable to command her legs to work. Rising from the chair to get away took too much effort.

CHAPTER TWENTY-ONE

DONE WITH a morning full of sales meetings, Eric walked to his car, finally able to pull out his phone. Too busy wooing new clients, he'd silenced it and hadn't had a chance to check his messages until now.

Eric placed his briefcase on the seat next to him and climbed inside. Smiling, totally satisfied with two signed contracts, he brought the phone to his ear to listen to the first of Simone's messages. He couldn't wait to share his good news. That he had someone who loved him was a miracle in and of itself. That the person was Simone was doubly miraculous.

He started the car and froze when her voice announced her plans. Glancing at his watch, he swore under his breath. She was already on her way.

In a quick move, he backed out of the space and sped toward the address she'd mentioned. While stopping for a light, he called in reinforcements. Hopefully Scotty could meet him there. His foot stomped on the pedal, increasing the car's speed. He rounded a corner a bit too fast but didn't slow down, praying he wouldn't get a ticket.

Eric hadn't dismissed Blaine Moorecroft as the person behind Simone's would-be kidnapper.

God in heaven, what we she thinking, going to his office alone?

<><><>

BLAINE STRODE into his office, halting in mid-step when he spied his brother's wife standing next to his desk. When he saw the bleary-eyed woman slumped in the visitor's chair, shock and confusion froze him in place for a moment.

"Sherlyn?" he asked, finally finding his voice. "What's the meaning of this?" More to the point, why was she now waving a gun?

"Ah, Blaine. You're right on time to meet your murderer."

"What? Are you flipping crazy?"

"I'm perfectly sane. Unfortunately for you, you picked the wrong wife all those years ago. Which is why you have to die." She pointed the gun at him. "Sit down and put your hands on the desk where I can see them."

"Because I didn't pick you?" Blaine cautiously moved to sit, eyeing her warily the entire time. "For that I have to die?" He shook his head. "I don't get it."

"I urged you to reason with your father to turn down the senate race, one you didn't even want, and give the opportunity to Kent. But no. You had to play the martyr."

"Blaine, I need—" Kent, who had just burst through the door, stopped abruptly. "What the hell?"

"Go away, Kent," Sherlyn said tersely.

"She's threatening to kill me," Blaine said, giving his brother a panicked look.

His mouth agape, Kent stared at his wife for a beat. "For God's sake, put the gun down."

"Not until I finish cleaning up one of your biggest messes."

Kent gave her a look of disbelief. "By threatening my brother?"

"Take a good look at the woman in the chair, and you'll understand why she has to shoot Blaine."

Kent did as she asked and shrugged. "So?"

"Don't recognize her?" When Kent shook his head, she said, "She had your baby."

That got Blaine's full attention. He studied the woman a moment and finally recognized her as Simone Harris, his worst nightmare.

"No," Kent said as Blaine shouted, "I didn't touch her."

Sherlyn pointed the gun at Blaine and said in a condescending voice, "Of course you didn't touch her. I was there nursing a broken heart after you dumped me, and I saw the entire scene unfold." Sherlyn clucked her tongue. "I wanted you, not your sniveling brother, who had to drug women to prove he could keep up with you. Kent drugged her and . . ." She waved the gun in the air. "Well, suffice it to say, as a result she had a kid."

"What? That's impossible." Kent looked at Blaine. "I'm sorry, bro. I didn't know."

"Did you drug her?" Blaine asked.

"No. She was already high," Kent said.

"Don't bullshit me!" Blaine jumped out of his chair. "You handed me the drink I gave her before I had to leave—" He broke off and his eyes widened. It all made sense now. "You raped her and let her think it was me?"

No wonder Simone had been so incensed and accusatory, so furious at him. Blaine had thought she was crazy, but now he realized she'd been a victim all along.

Just like him.

He started toward his brother. "Why, you—"

"Sit back down," Sherlyn shouted.

Blaine stopped short. Hands in the air, he did as she demanded. "Okay, okay."

"Sherlyn, you can't do this." Kent's glance was pleading.

"It's the only way you can rectify the situation and take your rightful place as a senator. You'll get the sympathy vote, and she'll take the blame."

"You can't kill my brother." Kent lunged toward her and grabbed for the gun.

As Kent and Sherlyn struggled for control of the weapon, Blaine used the diversion to rush to Simone, who was totally out of it. Hell, the bitch had obviously drugged her.

When the gun went off, its report shockingly loud in the confines of the office, Blaine froze.

CHAPTER TWENTY-TWO

A T THE same time the gunshot reverberated through Blaine's office, his outer door burst open and two men he'd never seen before rushed inside.

Sherlyn backed slowly away from Kent's slumping form, her face white with shock. Blood soaked his midsection, the red color contrasting sharply with the stark-white dress shirt.

"Kent." She bent over her husband as Blaine relieved her of the weapon and tossed it out of her reach. "He wasn't supposed to die." The look she gave Blaine was pure hatred mixed with madness. "This is all your fault."

Blaine glanced at the two men who'd stormed into his office. One had snatched up the discarded weapon while the other had rushed to help Simone. "Call 911," he cried out, and the man holding the gun set it on the desk and pulled out a cell phone.

He shoved Sherlyn aside, ignoring her crazy accusations, and knelt to cover Kent's wound with his hands, trying to staunch the bleeding. Even with no medical background, Blaine knew his brother's prognosis didn't look good.

"She's got the gun!" one of the men shouted.

Blaine snapped his head up to see Sherlyn put the revolver in her mouth. Before anyone could stop her, she pulled the trigger.

Kent flinched at the gun's report and sagged in despair at the sight of his wife's crumpled body on the floor near him. Looking up at Blaine, he whispered, "I'm sorry I messed up. Sorry I always wanted what you had."

Blaine blinked hard, trying to hold himself together as he frantically worked to stop the bleeding. "That's okay, bro. Just hang on."

"No, jealousy is never okay. It's ugly and—" Kent broke off and closed his eyes.

"I forgive you," Blaine choked out. "Please don't die."

His brother took a shuddering breath and looked up at him with a wan smile. "Thanks. Tell her I'm sorry for what I did to her." Then he went limp in Blaine's arms as the life ebbed from him.

Still cradling Kent's head and staunching his blood, Blaine fought back tears.

When the paramedics and police officers arrived, he stood aside to let one of the paramedics try to bring his brother back to life while the other dealt with Sherlyn's body.

His desk was splattered with her blood and . . .

"What a mess," he said in a low voice. Then he glanced at Simone, who was finally becoming more lucid. "What a goddamn tragedy."

Maybe if he'd taken Simone's accusations more seriously and done some investigating back in college, all of this could have been avoided.

He doubted the woman would forgive his brother—or him. Or his family, for that matter.

EPILOGUE

SIMONE HAD felt compelled to attend Kent Moorecroft's funeral. Now at the cemetery, she found a spot in the back of the somber crowd who'd gathered at the gravesite. The approaching storm clouds matched the setting and her mood.

Ashes to ashes and dust to dust . . .

The words echoed in Simone's brain as the casket containing Kent's body was lowered into the ground. Watching it disappear, she struggled for some empathy, but the only emotion she could muster right then was relief. Relief that a monster was dead. It wasn't lost on her that Kent's death saved her from a big mess. And his wife's death saved the taxpayers from a long and drawn-out trial.

Murder/suicide was how the Moorecrofts spun it for the press, which worked for her. Their rendition kept Simone and her daughter out of the news.

Simone's biggest worry now was how best to explain everything to Amelia. Obviously, the task required her to start at the beginning and be as truthful as possible. Yet, how would Amelia take the news that she was the product of rape? Simone had wanted to spare her daughter the sordid truth. Now that truth was even more sordid with the deaths of Kent and his wife.

Blaine was beside himself with guilt. He'd apologized so many times for not believing her. His father had also apologized profusely. Grief stricken and humbled, Clifton Moorecroft had admitted to knowing Amelia was a Moorecroft. He'd also guessed which son had done the deed, even admitted to figuring out it was rape.

Clifton had kept his wife in the dark about their younger son's true nature. Unwilling to besmirch the Moorecroft name with any kind of negative publicity, he'd paid Simone off.

As a result, Blaine's mother was just another heartbroken victim. She'd not only had to face her son's death, but the ugly truth about that son's actions.

Simone didn't have the heart to deny Senator and Mrs. Moorecroft access to their granddaughter, providing Amelia was okay with the idea. Her daughter was old enough to make up her own mind.

Besides, Clifton's main intent had been to protect his family. Maybe his head was in the wrong place, but Simone understood the need to protect loved ones. She also recognized the need to forgive them and let go of the past.

For her daughter's sake, she was more than willing to try. Not an easy task, but with Eric's love and support, she'd been able to take the first step in the journey by making her offer to the Moorecrofts. After all, Eric had forgiven his father for far worse transgressions.

Her thoughts traveled back to yesterday, when Eric had gotten notice that his father was in the final stages of death. Simone had accompanied him to Ronald Coleman's hospital bed and witnessed Eric show compassion and love to a man who clearly didn't deserve either.

Trish had said it best. "It's not for us to judge."

How true, Simone thought. Both men had met their maker. Let Him be their judge.

When the service ended, Simone heaved a weary sigh and glanced at the heavens. *Thank you, Lord, for the courage to let my own anger and bitterness go.*

Doing so relieved her of a heavy burden, also allowing her to grasp the full impact of her decision.

Forgiveness wasn't for the person who was forgiven, but for the one who forgave. It freed the soul and allowed positive emotions to blossom in the heart.

Hating the Moorecrofts all those years had held her heart hostage. Now that Simone had embraced forgiveness, the bounties of love, compassion, hope, and gratitude overflowed within her.

She glanced over at Eric and squeezed his hand, drawing his attention. The smile she offered held all that was in her heart. The gaze he turned to her was filled with the same emotions.

Together they could be a family and live happily ever after.

THE END

Thank you for reading *Hidden Agendas*. If you enjoyed it, please help others find it by posting a review wherever you bought it. I appreciate all reviews, whether positive or negative. Share a link, tweet about it, Facebook it ... everything helps in this interconnected Internet world.

If you'd like to know when my next book is available, sign up for my newsletter on my website, sandyloyd.com, or e-mail me at sandyloyd@twc.com and I'll add you to my list.

Follow me on Twitter at @sloydwrites, or like my Facebook page at facebook.com/sloydwrites.

If you'd like to read more of my work, turn the page for the first chapter of *Shattered Dreams*. It's an award-winning story that doesn't skimp on romance, and the hero and heroine fall in love while solving a mystery.

Excerpt of *Shattered Dreams*

It's all fun and games until someone dies

Claire doesn't miss her lying, cheating husband, but that doesn't mean she killed him. Someone else committed the crime and framed her for it, and she prays it was anyone but her twin sister—the only other person who had motive and opportunity.

Jason wants to believe Claire, but a lie of omission destroys his trust in her. Is she truly innocent and deserving of his heart, or is she seducing him to ensure he defends her? With doubts assailing him, Jason is determined to solve the murder, even if it means hardening his heart and pushing Claire out of his life.

Shards of lies and betrayal can shatter anyone's dreams, but her mistake just might destroy him.

Chapter 1

Claire Grayson Carter felt the warm sun on her face long before she dared open her eyes. When she finally did squint, brightness invaded and pain shot through her brain. Her eyelids snapped shut.

It took a while before she risked another attempt. This time she used a hand to block out the early morning light and opened her eyes hesitantly while she slowly sat up.

Moaning, she gripped the seat to still the subtle sway of the anchored sailboat. To fend off the offensive rays and to ease her queasy stomach, she bent over with her face in her lap.

"Oh God." Would the pounding in her head ever stop?

Why did I drink so much? That and the question about where her husband might be were her two most pressing thoughts.

"I should've never had that last glass of champagne," she muttered as another wave of queasiness passed. *Please, Lord*, Claire prayed, *get me through this and I'll never drink so much again.*

With shaky hands, she grabbed hold of the railing until a flush of perspiration passed. Then she pulled herself to her feet, taking deep breaths. Once she felt confident to move again, she raked trembling fingers through her matted hair. Resting her hand on the back of her neck, she scanned the calm seas.

A fish jumped. Its plop distorted the clear water for seconds. Eventually, the ripples fanned out and left the blue-green mirror intact.

Though her nausea had receded, little grenades inside her head hadn't. One right after the other exploded. She lifted her hand to rub the pain away, and saw red streaks along her arm.

Startled, she glanced down. Dark stains saturated her white silk shirt that hung unbuttoned. When she caught a coppery whiff, the distinct scent of blood, her scalp tingled.

Her heartbeat quickened as she took in the teakwood deck, where a couple of drained champagne bottles and two flutes were strewn about, along with the remnants of a gourmet meal.

She then focused on a red trail that led below. Another cold sensation washed over her despite the heat of the harsh sun. Her lungs seized, and dread rose up instead of air.

"Carl?" She tentatively followed the dark spots that increased in size down the stairs, to the galley and open salon below, where they just stopped in a small dried puddle in front of the stove. "Carl?"

She unlatched the door to the back berth. The bed was undisturbed, and the stowed nylon bags on the teakwood floor were exactly as she'd left them the evening before.

She pivoted and stumbled toward the V-berth as the forty-foot sloop lurched unexpectedly in the water. Gripping the door frame for support, Claire climbed on top of the bed's rumpled sheets in the center of the tiny room, pushed open the front hatch, and poked her head out.

"Carl?" she yelled at empty space. The quiet stillness of the morning was amplified as her heartbeat pounded in her ears.

Hysteria set in as another wave of nausea rolled over her, lapping at her gut like the sea hitting the beach. She dropped the hatch and had to sit a moment on the edge of the bed until the feeling passed.

The jackhammers in her head weren't helping matters any. Neither was the fact that she felt weak. The desire to exert any effort had completely deserted her. Through sheer willpower, she mustered forth every bit of energy she possessed and continued her search.

At the door of the head, she halted with her hand on the latch. "Stop! Get a grip." The sharp verbal reprimand worked like a crutch, and gave her the courage to open the door. Yet when she did, her fear expanded at the sight of a bloody hunting knife on the sink in the small bathroom.

She staggered two steps back, far enough to grab the galley stove, and sank onto the settee cushions next to it. Her gaze landed on the table a few feet away. The chart she'd used the day before still lay open where she'd left it.

Breathe. First one breath, and then another. Breathe.

"Okay . . . okay. Think." Claire peered unseeing out the window at the water beyond. Why couldn't she remember?

A few tears escaped and trekked down the sides of her face. Her memory was a blank slate after she and Carl had made love last night. Worse, the events leading up to that moment were blurry.

"Did I drink so much that I blacked out?" After whispering the words, she glanced around the open room. Nothing seemed out of place. Except dried blood.

There had to be a plausible explanation. Maybe Carl had a nosebleed and then took the inflatable to shore for a newspaper, and he just hadn't returned yet. He probably left her a message on her cell phone.

She jumped up from the coral-colored cushions, and avoiding the blood on the teak floor, rushed up the steps to the deck outside. Seconds later, she lurched toward the stern where her cell phone was stashed. Clutching the lifelines to keep from falling, she reached for her phone and brought it to life. No new messages were on the phone, either via text or on voice mail.

When her gaze flew to the stern, hope deflated as rapidly as an inner tube with holes when she spied their dinghy bobbing in the water. Her attention then moved to the port side. Their diving gear was situated in a straight line, exactly where they'd left it the day before.

She glanced out at the crystal-clear water and spent several minutes thoroughly searching the horizon and the area surrounding the boat. The sun beat on her neck. Birds screeched and fish jumped, disturbing the quiet and indicating a morning coming to life. But no Carl.

"Carl," she yelled.

Nothing! Claire worked to stop a fresh flow of tears and to push past her immobilizing fear as questions consumed her.

She needed help. Someone had to help her find Carl. She wiped away tears with her blood-soaked shirt, ignoring the implications, and slumped down onto the padded bench to call the police.

Spying the dried blood on her arm, she halted with the phone in midair. What would she say? That she'd woken up alone, all covered in blood, and couldn't remember?

With no other choice, she punched in 911, closed her eyes, and hoped for the best. "I'd like to report a missing person," she said to the operator.

After giving the woman specifics and being told someone would be there shortly, she ended the call, praying they would hurry. She'd never dealt with the police before. Considering the circumstances, the thought terrified her.

The quiet pervaded, adding to her isolation and her sense of impending doom.

Unable to simply sit still, she swiped the phone screen and hit a preset number.

"Hello?"

"Gwen?" Just hearing her best friend's voice calmed some of her fears. "Something's happened. Carl's not here."

"What do you mean, he's not there? Aren't you on a boat for a romantic weekend?"

"He's gone. What's more, there's blood all over. I can't remember what happened."

"Blood? Are you sure?"

"Of course I'm sure," she hissed, losing some of her hard-won control.

After blubbering for a drawn-out moment, she wiped her face and pulled herself together. She ran a hand through matted hair and felt what could only be dried blood. After a deep shudder, she inhaled and filled her lungs to capacity.

In a calmer voice, Claire relayed what had had happened since she woke, and finished with, "Gwen, I'm scared. There's a bloody knife in the head. I've called 911. But what if they think I did something? Or worse, what if I did? It's horrible not remembering anything. What do I tell them when they get here?"

Gwen Anderson remained silent. Claire could almost hear her efficient brain churning. The act brought a small turn to the edges of her lips as the stiffness in her shoulders relaxed. Calling Gwen had been the right thing to do.

Those thoughts stayed in place until Gwen's next words shot through the phone.

"You should call Crystal."

"No way. I can't." How could Gwen even suggest calling her sister? "I haven't talked to her in months, and I don't plan on doing it now."

"You sound desperate, and desperate times call for desperate measures."

"Not that desperate. Think of another solution."

Claire gazed out the bow of the boat. Sunlight glistened off the azure water as billowy white clouds floated aimlessly on the horizon. None drifted close enough to the sun to darken the morning.

The day looked to be another glorious one in paradise, except she felt as if she'd dropped into hell. Her head still hurt and she could barely think, but she hadn't lost all her wits. She was in no condition to deal with Crystal right then.

"Claire, she's an attorney. She can advise you."

"She's a divorce attorney, so I don't see what solutions she'd have in this situation." She'd rather have a root canal without drugs than talk to her sister, especially if the conversation involved Carl. For as long as Claire could remember, Crystal Grayson had always made Claire feel inadequate, and Crystal's mocking *I told you so* invaded her brain now.

"I'm betting she'd know what to do once the police get there." Gwen was quiet for a moment. "How about if I call her for you?"

"You'd do that?" The anvil of worry on Claire's shoulders disintegrated. *Thank God.* She knew she was taking the coward's way out, but she didn't care.

"I don't like her either, but I'll do it. Sit tight. I'll call you right back."

"Thanks, Gwen. I owe you."

While she waited, Claire paced, holding her hands to keep from fidgeting. Every now and then she'd stop to look out over the water, hoping for . . . what? She snorted. It wasn't as if Carl was going to rise out of the water after a long swim.

Where in the hell is he?

That sick, coppery scent rose up again, and she gagged.

Seconds later, her cell phone blared. Claire picked up on the second ring after noting Gwen's number on the caller ID.

"What did she say?"

"She's calling a friend."

"She's really helping me?" The incredulity in her voice rang out loud and clear.

"Yes, Claire. Crystal may be a bitch, but she's still your sister, for God's sake."

Delving into the dynamics of her demented relationship with Crystal wouldn't help matters, so Claire ignored the comment. "Who's this friend?"

"Says he's a good criminal lawyer and will know what to do."

"Can't say I'm not relieved."

"So am I. Listen, I can drive down and be there in an hour or so."

"No." Claire sighed and focused on a couple of dolphins frolicking off *Solitude's* bow. Every morning about this time, they swam past the sailboat. Her gaze fastened on the pair for a moment. As she watched, her breathing and heartbeat slowed, despite the stench and icky feeling of wearing blood.

"I don't know what good you'd do," Claire finally said. "But stick around. Let me talk to this lawyer. If I need moral support, you'll be the first to know."

"Okay."

Claire tried to smile at the bit of humor in the one word, but the slight curl of her lips fell far short of an actual smile as she punched the OFF button and resumed her pacing.

"Roberts here," he said in a groggy voice.

"It's Crystal Grayson."

Jason Roberts wiped his face and worked to clear his sleep-fogged mind. Maybe he hadn't heard correctly. He sat up and leaned against the wooden headboard.

"Crystal?"

"Yes, and don't hang up."

Since their last conversation over a month ago had ended heatedly, he was taken aback with the call and wanted to hang up, but didn't because he owed her. And one thing he knew about Crystal Grayson. She always collected her debts.

"Okay. You got my attention. So, why's the famous go-for-the-jugular divorce attorney calling me this early and at home? We don't go to court till the end of the month. My bill's paid, and as I recall, I made myself quite clear during our last discussion."

"Jason, I can't believe you're still pouting."

The exasperation in her voice made Jason sigh and shake his head. The woman on the other end was the most brazen person he'd ever dealt with. Her ballsy approach reached new highs, even when compared with some true dregs of society he'd encountered as a defense attorney over the years.

"Pouting?" He rolled his eyes. "Nice try. You know damn well why I'm surprised you're calling."

"Yes, I got that. Guess I'm particularly adept at surprising you."

"Understatement if ever I heard one."

"Who knew you were a lawyer with scruples? You have to admit my offer was an interesting one, and you were tempted. I saw it in your eyes."

"Let's not go there." He snorted. "I can't believe we're having this conversation."

"It would've been worth it," she purred, and tossed out a throaty laugh. "After all, a night with me in lieu of my fees seemed quite reasonable."

"They've got a name for that. Did you call to bring it up again, or do you have a purpose?"

Another throaty laugh shot through the phone, irritating him. Claws raking over a metal roof would have been an improvement.

"I do have a purpose. I realized too late I insulted you with my offer, but you said if I ever needed your criminal services, you'd reciprocate. I'm calling in the favor."

"What is it?" Jason sighed and rubbed his eyes with his forefinger and thumb. He didn't need this shit right now. But he still needed Crystal Grayson. Big time. At least until his divorce was final.

She went above and beyond. Worked her butt off to make sure he shared custody of his two daughters, who were now his life. In an attempt to punish him for having the audacity to require fidelity in his marriage, his soon-to-be ex-wife had threatened to call Seattle home and take his two girls as far away from South Florida as possible. Crystal had effectively stopped not only Elise's attempt to leave the area, but also her attempt to beggar him as well.

"I'm retaining you for my sister."

"You have a sister?" He tried to keep the surprise out of his words.

Somehow Jason had never imagined the viperous divorce attorney as a normal person with a family, but he surmised even serial killers had family members somewhere who loved them, so why shouldn't Crystal?

"She's my twin. Identical, in fact."

"There are two of you?" Jason swore under his breath. "God help us."

"Real funny! But seriously, I got a call from her best friend. She thinks Claire's in trouble. I don't know what to think, which is why I called you to check it out."

"Claire?"

He reached for the knob on the nightstand and pulled, but the antique drawer stuck. He'd have to work on that, he thought, yanking harder and almost knocking over the picture of Chloe and Amelia. As he righted it, his gaze hit the chaos of stacked backer board and bags of mortar scattered near his bathroom. He had a full day planned to tear up some ugly green linoleum. Hopefully, talking to Claire wouldn't take long.

He grabbed a pen and paper from the now-open drawer and began writing.

"What's her full name?" he asked. "And give me any pertinent information."

"Claire Carter." Crystal rattled off her sister's phone number. "She and her husband were out on their sailboat last night, celebrating. She woke up this morning and found blood all over the place. He's missing, and she has no memory of what happened."

"How convenient."

"No. The dickhead most likely cut himself shaving for a girlfriend who picked him up after Claire passed out."

"They sound like a charming couple."

"It's not what you think. She's the good twin, nothing like me."

He didn't miss Crystal's twinge of irritation his comment evoked, but couldn't stop from adding, "I'll keep that in mind."

"She's a lightweight when it comes to alcohol," Crystal went on, ignoring his taunt. "Also, she has a blind spot when it comes to her bastard husband. Knowing Carl like I do, I'm sure he took advantage of both. Look, personal issues aside, I'm worried. My gut instinct tells me something's not right. If my sister needs a criminal attorney, I want the best. You said it yourself many times, everyone's entitled to the best defense possible."

He couldn't argue with her logic, he thought, as she relayed more details. Cliché or not, he believed in truth, justice, and the American way, and valued integrity above all else. But having a good lawyer sometimes made all the difference in navigating the justice system.

"Gwen says Claire's disoriented and doesn't know what to do. Do you think you can help her?"

"The authorities need to be notified."

"She's already called 911."

"Okay. I'll talk to her. But that's all I can do unless she's charged with a crime. They may suspect foul play, especially with the blood. Might get ugly."

"Which is why I was hoping you could drive down and scope things out." She hesitated a heartbeat. "You're a sailor, right? I'd go myself but I hate boats, and I'm the last person my sister will listen to when it comes to Carl."

"You want me to drive to Key Largo?" He was unable to keep the shock out of the question, and his voice rose ten decibels. "From Boca Raton? Are you nuts? That's a four-hour round trip." What was the woman thinking?

"I understand it's asking a lot, but I'm really worried," came her anxious reply. "Carl's done something; I just know it. Claire needs an objective viewpoint. I'm betting there's no foul play, at least none involving my sister. She's too nice, too soft. Too goody-two-shoes."

Yeah, he mentally snorted. He'd heard it all before. Too many times. It was unlikely this Claire Carter was so lily white. Not after taking into account what he knew about Crystal. He'd bet a week's pay the two sisters were alike, leaves on the same tree. They were probably very similar in nature, especially when they shared the same genes and probably had the same upbringing.

Jason remained quiet as a gnawing feeling grew in his gut. He shouldn't get involved in any mess connected with the conniving woman. But he did owe Crystal, and his ex had the girls this week. Eyeing his master bath, he decided he could forgo a day of labor.

"I'll do it," he blew out on a resigned sigh. "Then consider my debt paid."

Jason said his good-byes and punched in Claire Carter's number, wondering if she'd stabbed her husband in a drunken rampage and woke with convenient amnesia. After listening to Crystal's description of all the blood, not to mention that the guy sounded like a jerk, he had his doubts about the twin's innocence. He'd defended numerous clients who'd done plenty worse for less motivation.

"Why me, Lord?" he murmured to himself as a voice

interrupted his thoughts. "Mrs. Carter? My name is Jason Roberts. Crystal said you might need my help."

"Oh, thank God. I don't know what to do."

Her genuine dismay set him back a bit. Jason hadn't expected the utter anguish in her voice. For some reason he couldn't fathom, the soft sound elicited some kind of recognition.

Yeah, right. Recognition of guilt.

"Calm down," he said in a soothing voice as he shook off the cynical thoughts. "I'm here to help. Crystal gave me a rundown, but I'd like to hear your version of what happened last night."

"That's the problem. I woke up covered in blood, and I don't remember much."

"Okay, then we'll start with what you do remember."

Jason took notes as he listened, stopping her from time to time to ask clarifying questions. Once he had all the specifics, they agreed she'd pick him up at the marina.

While writing down her directions, he said, "I'm driving from Boca, so it'll take me a couple of hours."

She murmured her thanks, and he added, "Outside of briefly explaining to the authorities what happened, don't answer any questions without me being present. Understand?"

A good offense was a criminal attorney's first rule of thumb for providing a good defense, if needed. Until he scoped out the situation as promised, she was vulnerable to law enforcement and their intimidation tactics.

"Yes. I understand."

"I'll call you when I get close to the marina."

After he hung up, he rose from the four-poster bed and wove his way around stacks of backer board and boxes of tiles for his ongoing house renovation while slipping out of his boxers. He yanked off his T-shirt and rifled through the bureau for fresh underwear, and grabbed Dockers and a sports shirt from the spacious walk-in closet that used to be a small bedroom.

Contemplating Claire Carter's story, he headed for the bathroom and turned on the shower before he stepped under the hot water. As warmth seeped into his bones, his mind spun.

What was it about her eerie voice that drew him? He discarded the thought, refusing to believe something so ludicrous. The circumstances surrounding the woman's situation intrigued him, not the other, and were definitely worth a trip. If anything, he figured he wouldn't be bored.

Hell, Jason thought while soaping up, he could handle the win-win scenario. He'd clear his debt with the annoying divorce attorney and be entertained in the process.

About the Author

Sandy Loyd has worked and lived in some fabulous places in the US, including Northern California and South Florida. She now resides in Kentucky and writes full time.

As a former sales rep for a major manufacturer, she's traveled extensively throughout the US, and has a million stored memories to draw from for her stories. She spent her single years in San Francisco and considers that city one of America's treasures, comparable to no other city in the world. The books in her California Series, starting with *Winter Interlude*, are all set in the Bay Area.

Sandy is now an empty nester who has written almost two dozen novels. She strives to come up with fun characters—people you would love to call friends. We all know friends have their baggage and when we discover what makes them tick, we come to love them even more.

Whether she's writing historical, time travel, romantic suspense, or contemporary romance, Sandy always tries to weave a warm love story into her work, while providing enough twists and turns to entertain any reader.

Other Books by Sandy Loyd

Contemporary Romances
The California Series
Winter Interlude – Book One
Promises, Promises – Book Two
James – Book Three
A Quickstep to Romance – Book 4
The Promise of Tomorrow – Book 5
California Series book 1, 2 &3
California Series book 2-4

Second Chances Series
Tropical Spice – Book One

Christmas Short Stories
A Christmas Miracle
A Christmas Miracle: The Gift of Love

Contemporary/Time Travel/Historical
Timeless Series
Time Will Tell – Book One
Games – Book Two
Temptation – Book Three
Timeless Series – Books 1-3

Romantic Suspense
D.C. Bad Boys Series
The Sin Factor – Book One
Raising The Stakes – Book Two
DC Badboys Series Books 1&2

Running Series
Running From Love

SANDY LOYD

Deadly Series
Deadly Misconceptions

On The Edge – 3 books –
A Matter of Trust, Running From Love & Deadly
Misconceptions

Stand Alones
A Matter Of Trust
Kicker's Legacy
Shattered Dreams

www.ingramcontent.com/pod-product-compliance
Lightning Source LLC
Chambersburg PA
CBHW071237130626
46556CB00003B/1051